"I'm a little out of practice."

Dylan ended his confession with a frown.

"It's okay," Nikki reassured him. "You want us to explore this...attraction, right?"

He nodded. "Interested?"

She swallowed hard. This was her chance to help him. Warmth filled her as she envisioned touching him, stroking him, bringing him pleasure...and peace. But something told her that leaving this man would be one of the hardest things she'd ever do.

She kept her voice casual, though her pulse pounded and her lips ached for more of his kiss. "Could be."

"I can't make any promises, Nikki. I'm not looking for anything serious."

"You mean no extras?" She laughed, knowing that they wouldn't be together long enough to worry about serious. "No frills? Sex only?"

"Well, I do owe you dinner."

With a boldness she didn't feel, she ran her hand up his torso. "Let's not put off until tomorrow what we can do today."

Blaze™

Dear Reader,

Have you ever met someone whose true-life story captured your interest like that of a fictional character?

I once met a young man who'd grown up with the Roma (Gypsies), saved a girl from an abusive household by running away with her, become engaged to her, then lost her in a senseless shooting. He was the first tortured hero I'd met outside the pages of a book and he inspired Dylan Cain, the hero of *The Morning After,* the first book in my SEXUAL HEALING trilogy.

Dylan captures the essence of the man who has loved deeply and now grieves the loss of that love. How could Nikki McClellan, born with the gift of sexual healing, not be drawn to him?

As always, it's a pleasure to share my stories with you. Feel free to write me at dorie@doriegraham.com or P.O. Box 769012, Roswell, GA 30076. Please visit my Web site at www.doriegraham.com.

Best wishes,

Dorie Graham

Books by Dorie Graham

HARLEQUIN BLAZE
39—THE LAST VIRGIN
58—TEMPTING ADAM
130—EYE CANDY

THE
MORNING AFTER
Dorie Graham

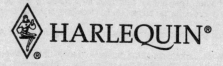

HARLEQUIN®

TORONTO • NEW YORK • LONDON
AMSTERDAM • PARIS • SYDNEY • HAMBURG
STOCKHOLM • ATHENS • TOKYO • MILAN • MADRID
PRAGUE • WARSAW • BUDAPEST • AUCKLAND

While writing this trilogy I reflected on the number of sisterhoods that have touched my life. Marion, Carol, Maureen and Cathy, this one is for you. I wouldn't be the person I am today without growing up beside you. Thanks for the support you've given me along the way and the love you continue to offer each day.

I'd like to offer a special thanks to Tami Harmon McGraw for her help and advice in portraying Nikki as a veterinarian. Thanks, Tami, for helping me keep it real.

RECYCLED PAPER · RECYCLED PAPER

ISBN 0-373-79200-X

THE MORNING AFTER

www.eHarlequin.com

Printed in U.S.A.

1

SHE WASN'T A ONE-NIGHT wonder after all. Euphoria filled Nikki McClellan Sunday morning as the aroma of fresh coffee and the clatter of dishes roused her from a languorous sleep.

This was a Sunday for the record books.

True to his word, Brad Turner was making her breakfast to celebrate their first night together as lovers. A profound relief poured through her. At long last, she'd kept a man until morning.

The intense Miami sun peered through a crack in the curtains. It promised to be another scorching June day, but today she could face anything. With a smile she slipped from the bed, then stole into the shower. Humming softly, she lathered herself, then let the warm rivulets rinse her. This morning her luck had changed. If she played her cards right, she might finally have the lasting relationship she'd always longed for.

As she exited the bathroom, she breathed deeply the scent of the bacon and eggs she could almost hear sizzling. Tying her robe snugly, she padded barefoot down the hall to the kitchen. Thank goodness neither of her sisters seemed to be stirring.

"You adorable ma—" She stopped in her tracks.

A tray laden with bacon, eggs, hash browns, fresh fruit, coffee and croissants graced the center of her breakfast counter. A folded sheet of paper sat beside it, her name scrawled across its front.

Brad was nowhere to be seen.

Disappointment choked her as she sank onto one of the bar stools. "Well, at least this one left a note."

Sighing, she unfolded the paper.

Dearest Nikki,

Last night was the most amazing night of my life, but I'm sure you get that all the time. No one has ever made me feel that way. Sex with you was like a spiritual experience, and I'm sitting here in awe, still trying to figure out exactly what happened.

All I know is that last night somehow changed my life. I feel as if I could go out and conquer the world. So that's what I'm off to do. I've never felt so sure of myself. You did that for me. You're a goddess and I only wish I was worthy of you. I will always cherish the memory of our time together.

With deepest gratitude,

Brad

"Gratitude?" She ground the word through her teeth. "Oh, hell, at least the man can cook."

"WOULD YOU LIKE SOME TEA and honey cakes, dear?" Sophie Patterson, Nikki's aunt, set a tray filled with the steaming brew and sweet-smelling cakes on the low coffee table before them the following Thursday.

Nikki rubbed her stomach. She'd managed to finish off the entire meal Brad had left, then she'd spent the rest of the weekend and a good part of the week eating through her misery. Still, she felt a little hollow, and the best place for filling up was at her aunt's. It was also the best place for getting advice.

She shook her head. "You'd think all this rejection would have spoiled my appetite."

"Actually I would be a bit surprised if you weren't hungry." The late-afternoon sun played across Sophie's loose hair, illuminating an ample sprinkling of white in the dark strands.

Nikki gave her aunt a curious glance but refrained from commenting. Though Sophie often spoke in riddles, she always had a way of easing whatever troubles might drop Nikki on her doorstep.

Cradling the warm mug, Nikki settled back into the soft cushions of the couch. It was a sturdy old couch, much like the house and Sophie herself. In a world full of chaos and constant moves, Sophie and her Victorian with its wraparound porch had long been a sanctuary to Nikki and her sisters, Tess and Erin. It was the closest thing to home the girls had ever known.

But not for long. Their days in the apartment they shared were numbered. The one thing their mother had done right was to set up an investment fund for each of the girls at birth. In spite of the stock market's many ups and downs, the funds still managed to accrue a tidy annual yield. With help from that, an unexpected inheritance and the income Nikki had generated since purchasing her animal clinic last year, she'd amassed a down payment and the excellent credit she needed to buy a home of her own.

She glanced at her watch. She'd have to leave soon to meet with her real-estate agent. Since Nikki opened the clinic half the day on Saturdays, she took off Thursday afternoons. For the past three weeks she'd spent her free afternoons house hunting. She hadn't had much luck in her search, but maybe today would be different.

Sophie settled beside her, nodding at her own cup. "It's a special herb blend. It'll chase those blues away."

Nikki breathed in the steam before taking a long swallow. She'd learned long ago not to ask too many questions about Sophie's brews. If her aunt said the tea would help, Nikki meant to drink every drop.

"I just don't get it," she said, her throat tightening. "Am I such a loser? These guys really like me. You know, I can usually tell what they're feeling…."

She stopped. Though Sophie had been the first one to point out Nikki's empathic nature back in the days of her childhood, they hadn't spoken about it much since then. Perhaps her aunt thought she sounded like some babbling fool.

"You're wondering why you don't know in advance that they're leaving."

"Well, actually, it's gotten pretty predictable. You'd think I'd get a clue."

"It isn't easy being empathic. Emotions can be misleading and fickle. It's difficult to tell what you're tapping into."

"What is it about me that sends them all running afterward? It isn't as though I'm trying to tie any of them down. I'd just like a guy to stick around for a little bit."

"You're looking at it all wrong. It isn't that they're rejecting you. It's that they're embracing the world and all it has to offer." Sophie set her mug on the table, then offered the plate of cakes. "Try a honey cake, dear. It'll sweeten your disposition."

Nikki frowned. She wanted to rave and cry. Life was so unfair. She couldn't seem to keep a guy, and Tess collected them like baubles. "I don't feel like sweetening my disposition. I want to scream. I'm a good person. I make a decent living and I don't think I'm so hard on the eyes. All I ask for is a little bit of happiness."

"Ah, that you'll have in spades, love."

Moisture swelled in Nikki's eyes. "When?"

Sophie patted Nikki's knee. Her shoulders heaved in a big sigh. "I guess it's time. I had hoped to coax that sister of mine into telling all of you girls, but she's always been a little…"

"Flighty? Fickle? Self-indulgent? You can say it, Sophie. It isn't as though I haven't figured that out for my-self." The bitterness inside Nikki grew.

She had managed to forget about her mother for a short period of time. Thinking of her now brought on a fresh wave of misery. If only Maggie had been able to settle for just one great love, Nikki wouldn't have grown up feeling like such a vagabond. Instead Maggie—daughters in tow—had roamed from lover to lover, home to home.

"You've never understood her, Nikki. She's a free spirit, it's true, but she's got a huge heart."

"That she wants to share with as many men as humanly possible?"

"Actually that's about the gist of it. But what you don't understand is that she has a special gift she's granting to each and every one of them."

"Oh, I know about her 'gift' all right."

"I don't think so. You don't understand. How can I explain it? You see, you have this very same gift, love, only in you it seems to be much stronger. It takes a little longer for your mother's magic to work, but with you…well, it seems you're a one-shot wonder."

"I could have told you that." Nikki stood, then began pacing. Her vision blurred, and she blinked to clear the unwanted moisture from her eyes.

"I don't mean that in a bad way, dear. It's quite a marvel, actually. I remember your great-aunt Emma was the same way. Does take some getting used to, but she lived a long, love-filled life."

"Getting used to?" Nikki stared at her aunt in disbelief. "You're kidding, right? Because I don't think I can *get used to* the idea that the rest of my life will consist of a string of one-night stands. I'll become celibate first."

"No, dear, that would be most unfortunate. You have a gift. To keep it to yourself would be a terrible mistake."

Nikki stopped to stare again at her aunt. "I have the mystifying ability to send men running from my bed. How can you call that a gift?"

"Sit beside me. I'm getting a sore neck looking up at you." Sophie patted the cushion.

With a shake of her head Nikki settled on the sofa again. Her stomach grumbled and she took a bite of cake.

"I'd wager that each and every one of them left hearty and hale and a world better for sharing your bed."

Nikki snorted indelicately. "The only one who left a note said he was ready to go out and conquer the world."

"Exactly." Sophie beamed.

"Well, great. That makes it all better."

"*You* make it all better. You see, the women of this family all share the gift." Grooves formed between her eyebrows. "The gift does impact one's life, it's true. Relationships can be very short-term, especially in your case, and that takes maintaining a certain attitude—the ability to let go when the time comes. The empathic nature can be a terrible burden. Seems the most damaged are drawn to us. But the reward…" Bliss lightened her expression. "Well, hopefully you'll experience it for

yourself. The reward is beyond description. It's price-
less to give so selflessly—to change a life or even save
one—with the gift."

"Sophie, you've gone on and on, but you haven't really told me. What exactly is this gift?"

Sophie took a deep breath and faced her niece. "I'm
surprised you haven't figured it out. It's the gift of sexual healing, of course."

SOPHIE WAS NUTS. NIKKI frowned into her rearview mirror
as she braked at a stoplight. Sexual healing? Impossible.
Ridiculous. Who'd ever heard of such a thing? Sounded
like the kind of harebrained excuse her mother might have
dreamed up, but how could Sophie buy into it?

Her aunt had been disappointed when Nikki had
scoffed at her explanation. Then Nikki had graciously
excused herself for her appointment. She was a little
early, but for some reason she found the possibility that
there might be a small bit of truth to Sophie's tale most
upsetting. Did this mean she was doomed to flit from
man to man, following her mother's rootless path?

God knows, Tess seemed headed that way. Erin was another story, though. Her romantic pursuits had been very
low-key up to this point. Yet Sophie had said they'd all inherited the gift. Would they all end up alone in the end?

Exhaling to rid herself of the unsettling feeling, Nikki
checked her directions before focusing on the neighborhood around her. The best way to combat this new upset
was to concentrate on putting down roots of her own.

And this area, Coral Gables, looked like a great place to do just that. She was meeting her agent at the first house they were viewing.

The house was in an established tree-lined neighborhood with wide boulevards and lots of green space. No wonder Coral Gables was called The City Beautiful. Even better, it was a short commute to her clinic and she'd always loved this area. Tess and Erin would, too.

Nikki drove past a curious mixture of colonial-, French-, Dutch- and Chinese-style houses, some with ornate entryways. This area certainly had a flavor all its own. A bicycle path wound alongside the road. She turned onto a quiet side street.

"This must be it. Five-eighty-nine Chestnut Lane," Nikki murmured to herself as she pulled up in front of a two-story house.

She glanced up and down the quiet street. Ginger Parker, her agent, was nowhere to be seen. Nikki left the engine running. Cool air hissed through the air-conditioning vents as the sun beat down around her car. Shifting forward, she peered at the house.

She liked it immediately.

It had a classic look, with bay windows across the front and wide dormers below the sloped roof. Barrel tile covered the surface and an archway to one side appeared to lead to an inner courtyard. Ferns, palm leaves and deep russet and gold flowers hinted at a garden beyond.

She started at a swift rap on her window. A stranger peered in at her. Blond hair swept back from his furrowed brow. Blue eyes narrowed on her. A myriad of emotions seemed to swirl in their depths, and foreboding swept over her.

Blowing out a breath, she rolled down her window. "Yes, may I help you?"

"You're Ms. McClellan?" A roughness edged his voice.

It veiled a deeper vulnerability. Though he was a big man—hearty and hale, as Sophie would say—he somehow seemed...not whole, as if he was broken inside. How this revelation came to Nikki, she couldn't say, other than the usual way she felt things about people.

And what she felt about this man drew an empathic rush from her heart. He carried a deep sorrow. It pressed him down with a crushing weight.

The stranger cleared his throat. She fumbled to remove her sunglasses, warmth fanning across her cheeks. She'd been staring. "Yes, I'm Nikki McClellan."

"Mrs. Parker phoned to say she's been delayed. I thought you might like to wait inside."

"Oh. You're the owner?"

He nodded briefly, his expression unchanging. "Dylan Cain, at your service."

She cut the engine. "Thank you, Mr. Cain."

Though he stepped back, she was all too aware of his solid presence as she exited the vehicle, then turned to fidget with the lock.

"She shouldn't be long. You can wait in the study or you're welcome to have a look around."

She walked beside him, her chin just topping his

shoulder. He was tall, over six feet. Her arms tingled as the sheer vitality of him shimmered over her. She caught his spicy scent and her pulse quickened.

"Is this really a courtyard?" Needing to put some distance between them, she veered away from him, nodding toward the archway. A riot of tropical flowers stirred in the slight breeze drifting through the opening.

"I wanted a home that brought the outdoors in. The courtyard and its gardens are a central feature." He led her into the refreshing coolness of the garden.

Nikki inhaled a sharp breath. Tall palm trees presided over much of the space, adding needed shade. A large fountain stood amid a circular garden in the courtyard's center. Water splashed and gurgled from an urn held by a laughing mermaid, while her sisters freed a wide-eyed fisherman caught in his own net. Small buds of yellow, red and orange danced all around the fountain's rim.

The four corners sported smaller gardens, each with its own theme. A kettle wind sock prevailed over what appeared to be a bevy of herbs. Tropical flowers peered between and around huge boulders of varying shapes and sizes on the far side. Another area paid homage to a stand of palms that shaded a cozy hammock, and the last paraded flowers in a rainbow spectrum.

"It's beautiful." She turned slowly in a circle, breathing in the sweet floral scent.

"Yes, beautiful." His tone was dark and fluid.

She faced him. Heat shimmered in his eyes as his gaze traveled over her. Awareness warmed her blood. Framed by the tropical garden, he looked like a predator ready to strike. She took an involuntary step backward.

He straightened and the moment passed. "Every room has a view of the gardens."

Sunlight filtered through the leafy canopy and winked off the floor-to-ceiling windows and wide French doors that must indeed usher the outdoors in.

"This is incredible," she murmured. "I'm surprised you can bring yourself to part with it."

The muscles in his jaw tightened. "It's time."

Again a feeling of empathy swamped her. She stilled the impulse to place a comforting hand on his arm. Whatever ailed this man, he seemed quite inclined to deal with it himself.

"Would you care to see the rest?" He gestured toward a pair of French doors.

"Yes, that would be nice, if you don't mind." She followed him into the main entryway.

Jewel-colored light splashed across the wall above her. Opposite, a stained-glass panorama stretched above the heavy oak doors, depicting a mermaid singing to a sea prince.

"Do you prefer to wander on your own or would you like the guided tour?" Cain asked.

Her glance fell across a side table adorned with an assortment of gilt-framed photographs. The delicacy of the table and its ornate trimmings seemed in contrast to the man's dark nature. A blond woman with an easy smile peered from one of the frames.

Nikki straightened, suddenly feeling very much like an intruder. "I'd like the guided tour…if I'm not keeping you from anything."

He gestured with a wide sweep of his arm. "This is the foyer."

Her gaze again gravitated toward the stained-glass window. The mermaid's wistful expression elicited a strange melancholy in her. Or did the image evoke the emotion in Cain and she was feeling it from him? Why would such a beautiful display cause him sorrow? She frowned. Being empathic *wasn't* easy.

She blinked inexplicable moisture from her eyes as his gaze pinned her. "Is it an original?" she asked. "I've never seen anything quite like it—or the fountain, for that matter."

"Yes. They were both commissioned."

He turned stiffly, and she followed him into the formal living room off to one side of the entryway. Here the contrast between the style of furniture and the man seemed even starker. High wing-backed chairs and sofas, dark claw-foot tables and delicate lamps adorned the space. Silk wallpaper with tiny rosebuds covered the walls, one of which featured shiny brass sconces flanking a large oil painting of a Victorian lady meeting her lover.

Nikki couldn't help but verify her suspicions. "You collect antiques?"

Though his shoulders remained steady, he seemed to sag somehow. "It would appear so."

"I'm sorry. It's just a little odd. You don't seem to be the claw-foot type." As if she had any idea what type he might be.

His gaze caught hers. For a moment a storm threatened in his eyes, then he cocked his head and seemed to relax. "Perhaps I'm not."

"Oh." She waited with bated breath, but he didn't elaborate.

Did the woman in the picture collect the antiques and knickknacks? If so, where was she now? Was she the cause of Cain's pain?

And exactly what would you do about it if she were?

The doorbell saved Nikki from further speculation. Ginger Parker arrived in a bluster of apologies and out of breath, her blue-gray hair tousled by the wind. "I'm so sorry I kept you waiting."

She patted her hair in place and turned to Cain. "Thank you for letting Ms. McClellan in."

He nodded toward the study on the opposite side of the foyer. "No problem. I was just working."

"Oh, well, we'll let you get back to it then. Don't mind us. We'll just poke around on our own." Ginger shooed him toward the study.

Dylan hesitated. His gaze swung over his prospective buyer. She was quite attractive with her brown eyes and coffee-colored hair. She had a sturdy build, not too thin, but she seemed unsteady at the moment. He'd made her uncomfortable somehow. She looked…upset.

"Ginger has been through already. She previewed the

house a couple of days ago," he said, wanting to reassure the woman. "You're in safe hands, Ms. McClellan."

"Oh, please call me Nikki."

"Nikki then." He extended his hand. "And I'm Dylan."

"Yes, Dylan it is." She placed her hand in his.

Warmth surged through him. Not just the tingling heat of sexual awareness—though that was there, too, which surprised him. Sure, on those rare occasions when Steven Benson, his lifelong friend, had dragged him out, he'd felt the odd passing attraction. But nothing like this.

Earlier in the garden, Nikki's lush figure and sparkling eyes had had his mind wandering along lustful paths he hadn't pondered in a very long time. Now her warmth enveloped him in comfort and ease. As he looked into her eyes, serenity such as he had not known these past two years descended on him. Her gaze softened, and he could no more look away than he could let go of her hand. He fought the alarming urge to sweep her into his arms.

What had come over him and who *was* this woman?

Ginger cleared her throat. "Shall we?"

Nikki glanced away, breaking the spell. She pulled her hand from his as pink blossomed in her cheeks. "Yes, of course. So far I love it. It's certainly more house than I'd anticipated."

"Let's start with the study, then we can let Dylan get back to work." Ginger ushered her client in that direction.

Dylan followed, staring blankly at the papers on his desk. What had he been working on? A haze clouded his mind. He turned and nearly collided with Nikki.

"Now this is *your* room." Appreciation shone in her dark eyes as she took in the solid-oak furnishings and cluttered tabletops. Papers and files pertaining to the fraud case he was working on covered nearly every available space.

"I...this is where I work when I'm home. I like it to be...utilitarian." In fact, it was the one room Kathy had had no interest in.

"Dylan's an attorney." Ginger rubbed her hands together. "He's defending Councilman Weatherby. Imagine, one of Miami's finest citizens on trial like a common criminal. You'll get him off, won't you, Dylan? I can't believe George has done a dishonest thing in his life."

"I'm not at liberty to discuss the case. The local media is having a field day with it as it is."

"Yes." Nikki cocked her head. "I believe I did read something about it. I'm sorry. I don't follow the news as closely as I should. I spend my days doctoring furry critters, then fall into bed exhausted at night. I don't know where the time goes."

"You're a veterinarian?" Dylan almost smiled, picturing the lovely brunette with her "critters."

"Yes, I am. I've always gotten along better with animals than people." She caught her bottom lip between her teeth.

It was a full bottom lip. Luscious. Made for kissing.

"Nikki has her own clinic in Bay Heights," Ginger said.

Dylan forced himself to look away from Nikki. Guilt filled him. What had made him think of kissing her? Had the woman bewitched him? He cleared his throat. "Bay Heights. That wouldn't be a far drive."

"No, not at all." Nikki turned to Ginger. "I'm anxious to see the rest of the house."

"Of course you are, hon. Dylan, if you'll excuse us…"

"Certainly. Make yourselves at home. Just let me know if you have any questions."

Nikki glanced back, smiling as they left the room, and he stilled the urge to follow. "Briefs," he muttered as he sat at his desk. "Where was I?"

He consulted the notes he'd been scribbling when Ginger had called. "Right, finance summaries."

With quick motions he punched a number into his phone. After four rings, the message center on the other end picked up. He waited patiently for the beep, then said, "Evelyn, if you have them ready, I could really use those summaries on the Weatherby finances. In particular, I'm looking for September and October of last year. Give me a call if you have them, or just fax them over. Thanks."

He exhaled and focused on the file in front of him, immersing himself in his work. The accountants were going over every detail, but he needed to understand where the councilman stood himself. Though all the columns in Weatherby's P&L added up, Dylan's sixth sense told him all wasn't as it appeared to be.

A short while later, Nikki's musical laughter floated down from the upstairs, shattering his concentration. He tossed down his pen. He had purposely left the office and all its distractions to work at home this afternoon. Now how was he supposed to get any work done with all of this racket in the house?

After another moment of staring blankly at the page in front of him, he gave up all pretense of working. He stood, then went in search of the pair.

He found them in the guest room. Sebastian, Kathy's orange tabby, had draped himself unceremoniously across Nikki's shoulders. Dylan paused a moment, not breathing. Since Kathy's death, the cat hadn't let anyone pet him; let alone pick him up—not even Dylan.

Nikki turned. Her smile faded. "Your housemate found us."

Ginger ruffled the cat's ear and he hissed at her. "Oh my, he hasn't any use for me, though he climbed right up there. Seems to have taken a liking to Nikki."

"He doesn't like most people." Dylan took a shaky breath. Showing the house was turning out to be harder than he'd expected. He stepped forward to take the cat, but Sebastian growled and leaped to the floor.

"Ow!" Nikki clamped her hand to her collarbone.

"Did he scratch you?" Dylan asked.

"It's nothing."

"It's bleeding." Ginger's eyebrows formed a deep V.

"Let me see." The softness of Nikki's hand plagued him as he moved it aside to see the double slash where

Sebastian's claws had marked her. "I'm sorry. I'll get something for that."

She waved aside his efforts. "I'm fine. It's just a scratch."

"He's overdue for a clipping. He doesn't like me handling him, and I've been so busy lately, I can't remember the last time I took him in for a grooming."

"He didn't mean anything. Bring him by my clinic. We'll get him clipped and clean for you." She smiled as the cat rubbed up against her leg. "I've always had a way with the four-legged kind."

"So it seems." Dylan suppressed the anger rising in him. Why should Sebastian's reaction to the woman upset him?

Or perhaps it was his own guilty response triggering his feelings.

"Well—" Ginger checked her watch "—if you've seen enough, I suggest we move along, Nikki. We have several more homes to visit."

Relief flooded Dylan. Thank God they were leaving. His insides had been in a tangle since he first laid eyes on that woman. Now he could get back to work and get on with his life.

Nikki turned slowly around the room until she faced him. Her gaze caught and held his, though her words were directed toward Ginger. "Oh, I don't think that'll be necessary. I believe I'm ready to make an offer."

2

SUNLIGHT STREAKED THROUGH the stained glass in a last burst of fiery intensity before the sun set that evening. Dylan clenched his fist, unable to tear his gaze from the fading light. Kathy had loved the window he'd had designed for her twenty-fifth birthday.

That last fateful night they had been leaving for a party his parents had thrown to celebrate his passing the bar. Kathy had stopped to watch the sun give up its last rays. "Oh, look. The sun's saying good-night."

She had refused to leave until the final bit of color had faded, her sweet eyes growing sadder with each passing minute. Then she had turned to him with a shrug. "It just isn't the same without the light shining through."

He'd swept his arms around her and kissed her. "Then I'll be your light until morning."

Her arms had tightened around him, her breath warm against his cheek. "You're always my light, Dylan."

God, he missed her.

He swallowed past a sharp ache in his throat, gritting his teeth against the loneliness that always overwhelmed him at sunset. How wrong they'd both been.

She'd been the light.

He closed his eyes. To his consternation, a vision of Nikki McClellan flashed through his mind. Her dark eyes beckoned him, filled with a promise he refused to acknowledge. He pushed the image away.

"No."

No one would ever replace Kathy. He had no intention of pursuing any kind of relationship with Nikki. He had nothing to offer her.

The doorbell rang. He straightened in the dark, hesitating before rising. His family never visited, and hadn't most of his friends gotten the hint and given up stopping by long ago? It was probably Steven. His old boarding school roommate was a diehard.

Steven had gotten married a little over a year ago. It seemed settling down into his own happiness made him more determined to drag Dylan back into the world of the living. The more Dylan resisted, the harder Steven tried. Guess that's what best friends were for.

Dylan yanked open the door just as the bell sounded again. Evelyn Rogers, a paralegal at his office and the woman his parents had always favored over Kathy, stood on his doorstep. A tall man beside her met Dylan's steady gaze while a streetlight cast long shadows across the porch.

"Why, Dylan, I was beginning to wonder if you were home." Evelyn looped her arm through her companion's. His dark hair played opposite to the platinum strands framing her heart-shaped face. "This is Nick Vancouver. I don't believe you two have met."

Dylan hesitated a long moment, then shook the man's hand. "Dylan Cain."

"I've long been an admirer of your father's."

Dylan's gut tightened. Too bad he couldn't say the same. His father was hell in a courtroom, but Dylan had seen too much of the man's private affairs to hold any kind of respect, let alone admiration, for him.

Evelyn peered past him into the darkened house. "Has your power gone out?"

Dylan flipped on the foyer light, then stepped back wordlessly. As much as it would have pleased his mother, Evelyn had never been anything to him. Why then did it aggravate him to see this man by her side?

"I just wanted to drop off these summaries you requested." She pulled a file from the briefcase slung over her shoulder.

"Thanks." He took it from her. "I would have had a courier pick them up."

She shrugged, her glance swinging to Nick, then back. "I wanted to stop by. No one's seen much of you lately. You burrow into your office at work, then you hole up here the rest of the time. I wanted to make sure you were okay."

Irritation grated through Dylan. "I'm fine. You needn't have troubled yourself."

"Well…" She shifted and tried an uneasy smile. "We won't keep you. We have to run anyway. We're meeting Nick's parents for dinner."

She twisted a large diamond on her ring finger. Inexplicably the knot in Dylan's stomach tightened at the sight of the ring. Evelyn laughed a nervous little laugh, holding up her hand. "Isn't it beautiful? Nick surprised me with it last week."

Dylan nodded, unable to utter anything intelligible. He should wish them well, but the words stuck in his throat. He'd never cared for Evelyn in that way, so why was her good fortune so hard to swallow?

Beaming, Nick pulled her to his side. "I'm pushing for a September wedding."

Pink tinged Evelyn's cheeks. "He's so impatient, but we're going to try."

"Ah, well…" Dylan let the words trail off. What was he supposed to say— That he wished them all the happiness he'd lost the night Kathy had slammed her car into that power pole?

Nick released his fiancée. "We're going to be late. It was nice meeting you, Dylan."

"Good luck," was the best Dylan could offer as he again shook the man's hand.

"Take care of yourself. I worry about you." Rising on her tiptoes, Evelyn placed a kiss on his cheek. "Don't be such a stranger, okay. You'll come to the wedding?"

He shrugged. "I'm not much for ceremonies."

Disappointment flickered in her blue eyes. "Well… let me know if you need anything else."

He nodded, then shut the door firmly behind them.

What he needed was peace and quiet. What he needed was not to be reminded of all the happiness he had no hope of ever retrieving.

"SO, EVELYN HAS HOOKED HERSELF a husband." Steven Benson's green eyes glowed in the dim light of Dylan's study late that Saturday evening. "That throws a monkey wrench in your parents' plan. I'm surprised your mother hasn't called to agonize over it."

Dylan grimaced. His mother never missed a chance to play the drama queen. He lifted a bottle and two glasses from a nearby shelf. He wasn't a regular drinker, but tonight seemed to call for it.

He handed Steven one of the filled glasses. "She's storing it up, waiting for the perfect opportunity to let loose. The more people to witness how I've failed her and take pity on her, the better."

"What made them think you'd ever go for Evelyn?" Steven shrugged. "She's all right, just not right for you. She's more like them. Surface."

Surface. The word described Dylan's parents to a T. Appearances were all they cared about. Image was everything. With her highbrow bloodline and Ivy League education, Evelyn would indeed add luster to the family reputation. Unlike Kathy, who'd made it to Harvard not through her family connections or bank balance but on the full scholarship she'd worked so hard to earn.

He gripped his glass, stilling the urge to slam it into

the wall. His parents had never accepted her. They'd upset her, driven her away that night.

"You look like you're ready to break something. Don't tell me you're unhappy about Evelyn."

"It's not Evelyn. I don't know. Seeing the two of them mooning at each other…"

Steven's eyes narrowed. "Yeah. Sometimes it's tough to take."

The fax machine in the corner rang, then kicked on. Dylan sat brooding while several pages printed. He pushed his chair back, then reached for what appeared to be a contract. Gritting his teeth, he scanned the pages.

"She's met my asking price." He glared at the contract and took a long swallow of Scotch whiskey, welcoming the numbness the liquor instilled.

Steven refilled his own glass. "You've got an offer?"

Dylan nodded. "This woman came by the other day. Said she was ready to make an offer. When I didn't hear back, I thought she'd changed her mind."

"Even at your asking price, she's still getting a deal. It's worth every penny." He leaned forward, his cropped red hair spiking upward, his gaze intent on Dylan. "It's not too late. You can back out of this. I know I've been pushing for you to get back into the swing of things, but I wasn't suggesting such a drastic change."

Dylan hesitated for a moment. Was he making a mistake? Why was it so hard to let go? His gaze scanned the paneled walls. "No, there's no going back. This is the only room I spend any time in."

"But, Dylan, this house…it means so much to you. I know that better than anyone. Imagine what you could do if you dedicated yourself. You're a natural. It's a masterpiece, a sign of real creative genius. To just let it go…"

Dylan waved his hand in dismissal. "I'm an attorney, haven't you heard? We don't create. We tear things down, argument by argument. Besides, I've finally earned the old man's grudging respect."

A scowl marred Steven's otherwise pleasant features. "It would do the old bastard good to have his plans go awry."

"He's *my* father. I'm the only one who can call him a bastard."

"Ha! They were calling him that way before you were born."

"Either way." Dylan gestured at the room. "This house was a phase. I only managed it with your help. *You're* the real architect. Besides, I'm good at what I do now."

"But are you happy?"

"I buried all my happiness two years ago."

Steven smacked his glass down on the desk. "Yes, it's been two years. When are you going to snap out of it?"

Dylan narrowed his eyes on his friend. He picked up the contract. With a furious scrawl he signed his name across the bottom. "There. I've sold the damn house. How's that for snapping out of it?"

Silence hung over the room.

Steven slumped back in his chair. "I do want to see you moving on. I just hate to see you sell this place."

"It's done. She wants to set the closing in a month's time. So be it."

"Not even a counteroffer? You should have asked for more."

He shrugged. "I'll pay closing. Let the witch have the place."

"Witch?"

An image of Nikki McClellan floated in Dylan's mind. "She must be one. That or…something."

"By 'witch' do you mean 'bitch'?"

"No, not that."

Steven sat forward. "I get it. So your buyer's a babe?"

Guilt still plagued Dylan, but the liquor had loosened his resolve. "When we were in the gardens, all I could think about was getting her into the hammock."

"Excellent." Steven nodded in approval. "This is definitely progress."

"I feel like I'm being…unfaithful."

"No! You're not. Kathy would want you to be happy. This is a good thing. You should act on those impulses. God, it's about time. Ask this witch out."

"I don't know what it is about her…."

"I think she's just what the doctor ordered."

"I'm not ready for a relationship."

"Make it a no-strings affair."

Dylan stared at his empty glass. "I can't believe a woman like her would go for that."

"It's a new millennium. Women like their independence. You won't know unless you ask. This is *huge*. Do you realize you've been like a dead man walking around here? You've been working way too hard. When was the last time you even thought about a woman? I'd about given up on you. I can't wait to tell Rebecca. She's been living for this day."

"Whoa. I said that I find this woman attractive, but I didn't say I was going to do anything about it. This *is* a big step."

"But you're giving it serious consideration. I can tell. You've got that spark back in your eye."

Slowly Dylan nodded. Maybe Steven was right. Anything was better than the agonizing tedium his life had become. "We'll see."

"THERE HE IS, ALL FIXED UP." Nikki handed the kitten to its young owner. "Told you we'd make him feel better."

"He's a big boy. He didn't even cry. Just like me. I didn't cry when I got my shots to go to kindergarten, right Mommy?" The six-year-old owner of the kitten beamed at her mother.

"That's right, sweetie."

"Well, Oliver's all set." Nikki scratched the cat behind his ear. A wave of calm flowed from the little guy as he gave a contented purr. "You ready to take him home?"

The child radiated with excitement. "Can we find him a special treat?"

"You got it, sweetie. Thank you, Dr. McClellan."

Nikki bade mother, child and kitten goodbye as she walked them out of the examination room into the waiting area. Several people sat in the chairs against one wall while Janet, her receptionist, talked quietly on the phone.

Nikki paused, absently nodding at something Oliver's owner said. A tall blond man stood with his back to them, bent over the sign-in sheet at the reception counter. Her pulse quickened. A familiar melancholy drifted to her, but it seemed different today than when last she'd experienced it—tamer somehow.

The man straightened, turning toward her, and she smiled, unexpected delight filling her. "Dylan, I thought that was you. What are you doing here?"

He nodded toward her groomer, Sarah Hendricks, who stood behind the counter, her gaze fixed admiringly on him. Sebastian made a feeble protest from her arms. "I decided to follow your advice and bring him in for grooming and nail clipping."

"Oh."

The man was a mystery. Had she imagined that heated look in his garden? He certainly hadn't acted on it. In fact, when he'd come upstairs during her tour of his house, she'd gotten the distinct feeling he'd been angry with her. Thank God he'd accepted her offer on the house.

"He seems happy enough here." He nodded toward Sebastian.

"He's in the right hands. Sarah will take good care of him."

Talking soothingly to the cat, the young woman finally tore her gaze away to head toward the grooming area. Nikki drank in the sight of Dylan. He wore a charcoal suit with a blue shirt that brightened the color of his eyes. His shoulders appeared broader, and he seemed to take up more space in her waiting area than he had in the expanse of his house.

His pleasure at seeing her swept over her, stealing her breath and warming her cheeks. She had never experienced this kind of intensity from anyone before. It was a desire so pure, her throat tightened with the beauty of it. It called to something deep within her, and she couldn't stop herself from reaching out to touch his arm. Even through his clothes she felt the connection.

"Thanks for bringing him in," she managed at last before dropping her hand.

"It was the least I could do." He traced his finger along her collarbone, sending a ripple of pleasure up her spine. "How's the scratch?"

"Healing. I've had worse, rest assured."

He nodded slowly. "This is a nice place you have here. Did I understand correctly that you own it?"

"That's right. I had a little help from my great-aunt Emma. She died last year and left an inheritance to my sisters and me. I could never have established my own clinic so quickly without her."

"It seems to be prospering."

"I'm doing okay."

"Okay enough to buy a house."

"Yes." She experienced again that giddy feeling that

had hit her when she'd heard he'd accepted her offer. "I'm really excited about that. It's my first."

The muscles in his jaw bunched, then relaxed. "Seems we both have something to celebrate."

She nodded.

He hesitated a moment, then said, "Perhaps we could toast our good fortune over dinner sometime?"

"Dinner?"

He was asking her out. The hungry glint in his eyes as they had stood in the garden flashed through her mind. So he had been interested. What would it be like to spend an evening with him? "I suppose that would be nice."

"Great. I…" A short laugh escaped him. "I have to check my schedule. I have to be in court quite a bit this week. In fact, I need to run now. My assistant will pick up Sebastian later, but could I call you?"

"I look forward to it."

"Wonderful." A smile lit his face.

"Nikki?" Janet walked over and handed her a clipboard. "Boxer and Mrs. Sneldon are ready for you."

"Thanks, I'll be right there." She turned to Dylan. "I've got to get back to work."

"Right. Me, too. So…I guess your number is on the contract?"

She laughed and it came out higher pitched than she'd intended. "That's right."

"We'll talk soon then."

She nodded, and he favored her with another smile

before turning to leave. She headed back to the examination room with a sigh. She needed to focus on her work before she succumbed to the worst case of infatuation in the history of womankind. Somehow she had to find a way to shield herself from this man.

3

"THE MELONS ARE FRESH TODAY. Would you like a squeeze?" The young man's eyes gleamed the following Sunday as he offered the fruit to Nikki.

His gaze dropped to her breasts. She shivered and pulled close the blouse she'd worn over her sundress. She'd seen that expression too often. She smiled politely and moved on, knowing she'd have to circle back for her bananas. Her best strategy was to put distance between her and this Casanova.

Sighing, she turned her cart down the juice aisle. Attracting men had never been a problem. If only she could figure out how to keep one.

As they had for most of the past week, thoughts of Dylan Cain swirled through her mind. She'd missed his call earlier. They'd been playing phone tag since his visit to the clinic, so she'd left her cell phone number on his voice mail when she'd last called him back. She placed a bottle of juice in her basket. Like the house, something about that man called to her.

Her cell phone rang and her heart quickened as she pulled it from her purse. "Hello?"

"Nikki, how's my girl?" Thomas Scott's voice crackled across the line. He was the one man who'd remained a lifelong friend of her mother's without ever having slept with her. Nikki loved him like a father.

"Hi, Thomas. Just grocery shopping."

"I hate to bother you on a Sunday…."

"No bother. What's up?"

"It's my sister's dog. He's got something weird going on. His whole face is swollen. He was fine one minute, then he just started puffing up like a balloon."

She frowned. "Poor Buck. Why don't you tell Lola that I've got to drop these groceries off, then I'll meet her at the clinic?"

"He's over here with me. I'm watching him while she's out of town."

"Oh, then I'll just stop by your place. You're closer than the clinic." And he wasn't far from Dylan's house. Maybe she could drive by afterward and get another peek.

At the house or the man?

"That'd be great. You think he's okay?"

"I have to see him first to know for sure. Was he outside when it happened?"

"We were out back. Why?"

"The last time I saw a dog do that, he'd just snapped up a bee."

"You think it's an allergic reaction?"

"Maybe. I'll know better when I get there."

"You are an angel, Nikki. I knew I could count on you to take care of this."

She said goodbye, then hurried to the checkout.

She made the short trip home in record time. With grocery bags weighing down her arms, she fumbled with the lock. The door swung open before she could turn the key.

Her youngest sister—green-eyed, blond-haired Erin—frowned at her as she grabbed several bags. "Why did you carry all this by yourself? I would have come down and helped—or at least sent one of the minions."

She nodded toward the back of the apartment, where a steady banging sounded. Tess's ex-lovers tended to hang around long after the loving. "Brandon or Brendon or whatever his name from the catering company is back there fixing her closet organizer."

Waving aside Erin's concern, Nikki pushed into the cozy living room and continued on to the kitchen. "I'm fine. Did anyone call for me?"

"Not that I know of." Erin followed Nikki into the kitchen.

"Is Tess here?"

"Her latest stud picked her up hours ago." Disdain laced her sister's voice.

Nikki flinched. She'd been a little down on Tess for following in their mother's footsteps, but in light of her talk with Sophie, maybe they should cut their sister a little slack. "You know, Erin, I think I understand her a little better now. I have to run help Thomas, but maybe when I get back we can talk about it."

An indifferent shrug was her only answer.

Sighing, Nikki set her load on the kitchen counter, then ditched her blouse. "You sure no one called? There weren't any messages on the answering machine?"

"I'm sure. No one called. What's up?" Erin asked as she dropped a head of lettuce into the vegetable bin in the refrigerator.

Nikki bit her bottom lip. Not wanting to get their hopes up needlessly, she hadn't mentioned her house hunting to her sisters in case the deal fell through. If she told her sister about Dylan, she'd want to know where Nikki had met him. "Nothing, really."

Erin eyed her for a minute, then shook her head and tossed an empty grocery bag into the recycling. She looked as though she might argue but continued putting away groceries, slamming cabinets harder than normal. Nikki would soothe Erin's rumpled feathers after the house was theirs. Her sister had been so moody lately, but Nikki would have to deal with her another time. If Buck really was having an allergic reaction, it could be life threatening.

Nikki hurried to Thomas's house. He was sitting on his front stoop with his sister's dog when she pulled up.

"What are you doing baking yourselves out here?" she asked as she climbed the front steps, medical bag in hand.

"Once I told him you were coming, he insisted." Thomas nodded his gray-streaked head toward the dog. "He seems to feel okay."

Poor Buck. His face was swollen and wrinkled like

a shar-pei's. Nikki knelt before the beast. The old Irish setter thumped his tail. "That's my boy. Did you snap up a wasp? Can I take a look?"

He whined softly as she pried open his mouth. "There's the stinger." Grabbing an instrument, she pulled the offender from his mouth, then patted him reassuringly. "Just a couple of shots and you'll be right as rain."

Worry lines crossed Thomas's forehead. "Will he be okay by the time my sister gets back tomorrow?"

"Let's take him inside and I'll get the injections ready. Give him about an hour and he'll be fine."

"Sure looks awful."

"Untreated, it could constrict his trachea or make his tongue swell so much it could cut off his breathing."

"So let's get on with those shots. That sister of mine will skin me if I return him damaged."

"Come on, boy." She urged Buck into the house after her.

A short while later, she found Thomas tinkering in the small workshop he kept at the back of his garage. A box fan stirred the thick air around him. He turned as she approached.

"Hey, there, pull up a chair." He patted the stool beside him. "How's the old boy?"

"Took his shots like a trooper."

"Thanks for the house call, pumpkin. Tell me, what do I owe you?"

She waved her hand in dismissal. "The way I see it, I owe you. I wouldn't even have the clinic if you hadn't talked me into going to work for Doc Emerson way back when. And I might not have stuck it out if you weren't constantly encouraging me and sending me business."

"Doc knew his practice would be in good hands when he sold it to you."

"It's certainly made life easier, stepping into an established practice. I'd be lucky to break even if I were starting from scratch."

"You've worked your ass off for it and you earned every penny. You helped build that business. Now, you send me a bill. Nobody makes house calls these days."

"This really is closer than the clinic. Besides, this way I can drive by the house I'm buying."

"You found a house?"

"It's in Coral Gables. The closing is scheduled for the end of July."

"That's wonderful! My Nikki is going to have her own home at last." His eyes misted. "I'm proud of you, girl. No one's worked as hard as you have. I've never known a more deserving soul."

Happiness filled her. "I've wanted this my whole life, Thomas. You can't know what it means to me. After this move, I'm never going to move again."

His eyebrows drew together. "I know living with Maggie wasn't easy, but it's made you strong and independent. It's made you the woman you are today."

"Aw, it wasn't so bad—not if you don't mind changing addresses every couple of months." In spite of Sophie's revelation, Nikki couldn't keep the sarcasm from her tone. "There was that one time we got to keep the same phone number through three moves. As long as I didn't invite any of the kids over, they didn't realize we had moved and I was spared the jokes about Mom taking a new lover. That subdivision had lots of street parties, so we met most of our neighbors. If there had been more single men, we might have stayed in the area a little longer." Bitterness tinged her voice. "Until I got my first apartment, I never knew what it was like to not live out of suitcases and boxes. That was life."

"You still don't understand her. She loves her art and her men."

"What's to understand? Sophie says Mom has a big heart."

"It's true. Do you doubt that Maggie loved each and every one of those men?"

"I don't know. I guess she did."

"Was there ever fighting? Any bad partings?"

"Of course. What home goes without fighting?"

"Maggie had fallings-out with her men? They fought?" Thomas peered at her, his eyebrows arched.

Nikki frowned. Funny, she and her sisters had had their share of sibling rivalry. Seems she and her mother had fought all the time. But try as she might, she couldn't remember a single moment of discord between her mother and any of her lovers.

"It's weird. I can't remember any. That seems strange, doesn't it, that all those relationships were peaceful, then the breakups amicable?"

"That's my Maggie. She has a special magic."

"Sophie calls it a 'gift.' I guess that's one way of looking at it."

"I take it you don't believe in this gift?"

"The gift of sexual healing? Get serious."

"Oh, Nikki, it's very serious business indeed."

She turned to face him more squarely. "You mean you believe my mother runs through lovers like last season's fashions because she's in their lives to heal them sexually, then she moves on once the healing's complete?"

"That's right. You do understand."

"No. I don't get how a man as reasonable as you can believe that."

"I don't get how a woman with this special gift can deny the magic she's been born with."

She stared at him a moment. First Sophie, now Thomas. Was there something to this after all? "So you believe this gift is inherited by all the women of my family?"

"That's my understanding, but you should be able to answer that for yourself."

A small groan escaped her. Tess certainly seemed gifted when it came to the opposite sex. With Erin it was hard to tell, but she was young still and hadn't had many serious relationships. Nikki's own love life was at least unusual. "I don't know, Thomas. It's just a little out-there, isn't it?"

"Is it?"

A shrug was all she could give in answer. "I suppose the empathic nature goes hand in hand."

"I believe it's stronger in some of you than in others." His gaze pinned her. "Could be worth exploring."

If it were all true, was she doomed to live a life devoid of love? "You mean, I should enter relationships for the sole purpose of healing but never get attached because I'll always have to let go?" Her throat tightened.

"No, sweetie, here's where you don't understand. Look at Maggie. She loves each and every one of them heart and soul. That's where the real magic comes from. That's where she taps into her healing potential."

"She loves them, then when it's over she just lets them go?"

His head bobbed. "It's the releasing that frees her to receive again."

"So does she just stop loving them?"

"Of course not. She has unlimited potential to love in that big heart of hers. It's part of her charm."

"But I don't want to keep getting left behind."

"Then be the one to go out and embrace the world."

"I don't know." Dylan's image wavered in her mind. If ever a man needed her healing, he was the one. She didn't question this inner conviction. And she'd never felt such a strong attraction. Did she dare explore her gift with him? Then, if she did, would she be able to let him go? "It's a lot to think about. For now, I need to get going. There's a house I've got to go see."

"A new house and a new life, Nikki."

She smiled. "Yes, I think so."

NIKKI'S HEART POUNDED AS she passed slowly in front of the house. Soon it would be hers. It stood as solid and enchanting as it had before, the stained glass over the door reflecting the late-afternoon sun.

"I'll just drive by," she murmured to herself.

An orange cat suddenly streaked in front of her. She slammed on her brakes. She came to a screeching stop, her front tire grazing the curb. To her amazement, the tabby, which looked suspiciously like Dylan's cat, jumped up onto the hood of her car.

"You little rascal." With a shake of her head she got out, then walked to where the animal stood meowing at her. "What are you doing? Were you trying to kill us both?"

"Well, hello, Nikki." Dylan's deep baritone startled her.

The sun danced across his bare chest as he approached. He wiped his hands on a rag sticking out of his shorts pocket. Apparently he'd been working in one of the gardens.

Warmth filled her cheeks and her pulse quickened. "I was actually in the neighborhood, not five minutes away. A friend of mine has a dog I had to see whose face was all…had to give him some injections… Anyway, I just wanted to drive by to make sure I hadn't dreamed this place. I tried to call you back…and your cat came out of nowhere."

She closed her mouth, her cheeks burning. She'd turned into a babbling idiot.

"Sebastian, bad boy." He turned his gaze to her. "I'm so sorry. I didn't realize he'd gotten out. Come on, big fella." He reached for the cat, but Sebastian growled, flicking his tail in warning.

"That's no way to act." Gently she stroked his back and he calmed. "Would you like me to put him inside? I don't think he'll mind if I pick him up."

"I guess I can't leave him out here to endanger other drivers."

The cat meowed when she scooped him into her arms but didn't resist as she moved toward the house with him. "Now, what was that all about? Do you have a death wish?"

"Could be. He hasn't been right since…for a while."

She nodded, her heart swelling. What had happened to upset Sebastian? Was it the same something that had put that wounded look in Dylan's eyes? The sun beat down on them as they crossed the wide lawn. Heat shimmered in the thick air.

Nikki stumbled, bumping into Dylan. "Excuse me."

He steadied her, the muscles of his shoulders rippling across an expanse of bronzed skin. "No problem."

With an effort she continued walking, all too aware of his musky scent and virile presence. And of the ache deep in his heart. She frowned against the overpowering need to soothe his pain. If she were to get involved with him, she'd best do it quickly, then move on. She was already too taken with the man. She was bound to get attached if she extended their acquaintance any longer than needed.

He kept his hand at her elbow, steering her toward the gardens. "The front door is locked. We'll have to go through the courtyard."

The cool green of the palm trees gave some respite from the heat as he stopped in front of the French doors. He opened the door but remained close. A cool blast of air hit her as she leaned in to drop Sebastian on the Spanish tile.

"You stay in here, away from the cars," she said, drawing a deep breath and trying to calm her heart. The cat gave her a backward glance before padding off.

"Would you like to go in and get out of the heat?"

She straightened. All the blood rushed from her head in a dizzying swirl. She reached out to catch her balance and her hand connected with smooth, hot skin and firm muscle. For a moment she stared at him transfixed, his heart thudding beneath her palm.

His gaze dropped to her mouth. She inhaled a shaky breath and pulled back her hand. "Excuse me. The heat doesn't usually affect me like this. Maybe I'm just dehydrated."

"Let's get you something to drink." Though she had regained enough of her equilibrium to walk, he kept his hand at her back as he guided her into the kitchen. The heat of his fingers branded her where the sundress bared her to his touch.

"I'm sorry to trouble you," she said as he filled two glasses with filtered water. "I never meant to intrude. I really intended just to drive by."

He handed her a glass and drank deeply from his own. "It's no trouble. I needed a break."

She downed half her water before daring another peek in his direction. The man was hairless and sleek, sculpted like a Greek god. She pressed the cool glass to her cheek. She had to get a grip. "You were working in the garden?"

"Weeding mostly. I have a lawn service that takes care of it. I just like to get in there sometimes. It's cathartic to yank up those weeds."

She nodded, not sure how to respond. A moment of silence fell and she set her empty glass on the counter. "Thanks. I feel much better."

A gust of cold air flowed over her as the air conditioner kicked on. Gooseflesh rippled up her arms, and her nipples beaded beneath the thin fabric of her dress.

His gaze traveled over her, lingering at her breasts before moving up to her eyes. "Would you like to sit down for a while? You probably shouldn't get back out in that heat just yet."

"No. I'm fine, really. I should be going." She cast a quick glance down. The halter top of her dress left little to the imagination.

"Would you like to tour the house one more time?"

Though her earlier excitement about the house stirred, she felt exposed. She folded her arms over her chest. "Maybe another time."

Disappointment swirled in the blue depths of his eyes. "Sure."

"But I'd love to see the gardens again."

He nodded and took her hand. "This way then."

His grip was firm and strong. Walking hand in hand with him as they strolled the stone path circumventing the far flower garden felt oddly right. He pointed out various flowers, but her pulse throbbed in her ears, making it difficult to hear him. His mouth was beautiful to watch as he formed each sensuous syllable.

What would it be like to kiss him?

"Don't you think?" He looked at her expectantly.

She bobbed her head in a half nod.

"I had a friend who didn't think so, but I know it'll hold two comfortably." He gestured to the large hammock nestled beneath tall palms.

Tugging her hand, he drew her closer to the hammock. "I've never been able to get anyone to try it with me."

"Oh." She turned to him. "You're awfully big."

"It's a double. It's supposed to be for two."

"Well, I'm sure two people fit then."

They stood for a moment in silence, then he brought her hand up. "No rings."

"No."

"No fiancé, then?"

"No."

"Boyfriend?"

"No, there's no one. I wouldn't have agreed to go out

to dinner with you if I was seeing anyone." Her heart thudded dully.

"Of course." His eyebrows furrowed. "Still, how can that be?"

"Well, guys just don't seem to stick around."

"That makes no sense."

"True nonetheless."

"But you're successful…and so beautiful."

She cast her gaze downward, and he hooked his finger under her chin, urging it upward. She shivered at the intensity in his so-very-blue eyes. "Truly beautiful."

He was going to kiss her.

The realization rang through her like a shot. The urge to flee took hold of her, but she stood, unable to move. His lips brushed over hers in a caress that grew steadily more demanding.

She opened to him, meeting the hungry stroke of his tongue, melding her body to his as he skimmed his hands over her back, then down her hips. Angling his head, he pulled her closer as he mated his mouth more firmly with hers, stealing her breath and sending heat rolling over her.

At long last he pulled back, his eyes blazing. "So…"

"So…"

"Um, I'm not great at this and I'm a little out of practice."

"It's okay. You…want to explore this…this attraction."

He nodded slowly. "Interested?"

She swallowed hard. This was her chance to help

him. Warmth filled her as she envisioned touching him, stroking him, bringing him pleasure…and peace. But something told her that leaving this man would be one of the hardest things she'd ever do. For some inexplicable reason, the prospect filled her with sadness. She barely knew him. How could she feel this way already?

She kept her voice casual, though her pulse pounded and her lips ached for more of his kiss. "Could be."

His brow furrowed. "I can't make any promises. I'm not looking for anything serious. You should know that up front."

A rueful laugh escaped her. She tried to squelch the bit of disappointment that surfaced. "You mean no extras? No frills? Sex only?"

"I owe you dinner. We could go out. It's up to you."

She'd been down that road too many times before. She and Brad had dated for three weeks before she had finally slept with him. The outcome had been the same. With the way she felt about Dylan in the short space of time since they'd met, only disaster lay that way. Better not to get too close. "I don't need any frills."

He nodded slowly.

With a boldness she didn't feel, she ran her hand up his torso. "Let's not put off until tomorrow what we can do today."

"We don't have to do this now if it's too soon. We could go to dinner first, then see how you feel."

"I'm not hungry…at least not for food."

He moaned softly and crushed her to him, claiming her mouth once more.

4

NIKKI'S MOUTH TEMPTED Dylan as nothing ever had. A shudder ran through him as he swirled his tongue with hers. His blood warmed. The feel of her. She shifted, her breasts heavy against his chest.

At long last, he pulled back, gazing down at her. That same feeling of serenity he seemed to feel at her touch flowed over him, but this time it was accompanied by a fierce hunger. *Lust.* He'd been without a woman for too long. He cupped the back of her head and drew her toward him until his mouth found hers again.

He'd never wanted to linger over a kiss, but the insistent stroke of her tongue held him captivated for long moments. He angled his head and ran his hand down her back, then around the side to her breast. It was firm and round, filling his palm. She shifted, giving him more room as he kneaded her. Her nipple hardened between his fingers, straining against the thin fabric. He rolled the pointed tip.

Without breaking the kiss he slid both hands down over the tight swell of her buttocks. He massaged her for a time, then lifted her so his stiffening sex rubbed against the juncture of her thighs.

Moaning softly, she ground against him. Her fingers stroked down his chest, toying with his nipples, further arousing him. She broke the kiss, moving her mouth along his jaw to his ear. "Should we try out the hammock?"

"Yes." He scooped his arm under her knees, then carried her the short distance. Balancing her, he shifted carefully into the hammock, settling her across his lap.

Her gaze darted to the open archway. "We're tucked away in the corner. I don't guess any passersby will see us."

"We can go inside."

She bit her bottom lip, her gaze dark and intent. "It's kind of exciting here. I've never done anything like this before."

"Neither have I." Oh, but he'd wanted to—that first day they'd met.

"We could always get started here, then move inside later."

"We could."

"You have a magnificent chest." She ran her palms over him, then dipped her head and took one of his nipples into her mouth. She suckled him while he fisted his hands in her hair and tried to breathe, the pleasure almost too intense to bear.

At last she nuzzled to his other side, but he gently urged her upward. "I think I'd like it better if I could do that to you."

"Oh."

"Would you like that?"

In answer, she reached up to the nape of her neck and unfastened her dress. Slowly she lowered her halter top. He took a deep breath and cupped one full breast, weighing it in his hand. He stroked his thumb over her peaked nipple. She had large areolas that begged to be sucked.

"Perfect," he murmured as he shifted her to lie beside him.

Keeping one foot on the ground to steady the hammock, he leaned over her and kissed the swell of her breast before brushing his lips over its center. She sighed, arching upward.

Every nerve ending in his mouth registered the exquisite softness of her skin, the pressure of her hard nipple against his tongue as she moved beneath him. Her soft cries of pleasure sent heat rippling through him. He'd never expected this when he woke that morning. What a gift she was.

When he'd had his fill of one breast, he kissed a path to its twin while she caressed his shoulders, chest and arms. The little sounds of pleasure she made spurred his excitement. Pulling hard with his mouth, he grazed her with his teeth and kneaded her firm flesh. He took his time, savoring each delicious pass of his tongue over the erect bud.

Nikki gasped, and the scent of her arousal drifted to him. He slid his hand up her thigh, pushing her dress aside as he went. His fingers brushed satin. Continuing his tender assault on her breast, he ran his fingertips along her cleft, feeling the wetness through her panties.

She shifted her knee, opening to him as he slipped his hand beneath the elastic. She was slick and swollen and hot. He explored her with his fingers, tracing her thick folds before circling her clitoris. He teased her, touching her lightly, then moved his fingers back to slip inside her.

She was surprisingly tight as her muscles clenched around him. He stroked her, spreading her liquid heat over her entrance and around her clit, before delving two fingers back into her passage. The elastic cut into his wrist.

He gave one last pull on her breast, then slid down her body. "These have got to go."

The hammock rocked gently as he slipped off her panties. He devoured her with his gaze. Her face was flushed, her eyes dreamy and her lips full and inviting. Her lovely breasts rose with each breath, her nipples hard and wet from his loving. And there the center of her femininity lay before him, her nether lips swollen and her clit engorged. Her sweet entrance glistened with her desire.

"You look like you want to gobble me up." She leaned forward to place her hand over his crotch and squeezed gently, then slowly pulled down his zipper.

"Well, that *was* the plan, but…" he said, his voice rough.

He settled back, letting the hammock rock as she

peeled aside his shorts. With deft movements she worked his erection free of his briefs, her fingers hot around him. His breath caught as she glided her hand up his length.

"Maybe I'll gobble *you* up instead." A streak of sunlight danced across her dark hair, picking up red highlights. Her breath was warm against his abdomen, her hair brushing his thigh as she moved down his body.

She circled one hand tightly around the base of his cock while the other slipped inside his briefs to cup him.

Her sweet lips closed over him and he groaned, unable to look away from the sight of his erection disappearing into her mouth.

Her tongue circled his tip, tracing the rim, then darting over the sensitive head. As if he were a rare delicacy, she savored him. Heat raced outward from his center.

When he thought he could stand it no longer, she released him, her eyes gleaming with a naughty light. But instead of moving away, she nuzzled him playfully, then kissed him. Starting at the base, she worked her way up his length, her lips and tongue working havoc over his flesh. Only after covering every inch did she at last feast on the head, dipping her tongue to lick the salty drops from the tip.

"You *are* a witch." He reached out to her. "How's a man supposed to take all that?"

"With a smile."

"I only have so much control."

"Sorry. I was really enjoying myself."

"Don't apologize. We can find other ways for you to enjoy yourself."

"I'm sure we can." She kissed him and he stretched back, pulling her with him.

Nikki settled herself on top of Dylan, straddling him and nestling her cleft against his hardness. Her body hummed with wanting. It was as if his desire fed hers, intensified it. And he desired her. His need radiated out to her, drawing her as no man ever had.

His lips were soft, but demanding, his tongue relentless in its pursuit. Her breasts grazed his smooth chest and he took her nipple between his fingers, rolling it, tugging it. The sensation rippled down to her sex. Liquid heat seeped from her.

She rubbed herself along his length, spreading her wetness over them both, while his mouth held hers in a heated ritual of mating tongues and teeth. He felt so good beneath her as she rubbed over him, her hips moving of their own volition. As the fire in her spread, she broke the kiss, pushing her torso upward while she pressed against him, her clit burning.

"Nikki."

She threw her head back, stroking faster and faster over him, her breath catching in tiny puffs.

"Damn, Nikki…"

Pinpoints of light flashed all around her. Heat spread through her like wildfire. She ground against him, circling her hips and pressing her hands into his shoulders.

She made one final thrust upward, her clit brushing his tip. He moaned, his body stiffening.

She cried out, gripped in an orgasm, vaguely aware of him shuddering beneath her, his hands tightening on her arms. For a long, heartrending moment she hovered in a place of infinite bliss while waves of release flowed over her in a seemingly endless spasm of pleasure.

At last she collapsed on top of him. He clenched his arms around her, fisting one hand in her hair. His breath fanned her cheek. After a time, his hold loosened and she shifted to look at him.

He gazed at her from under sleepy lids. "You know how to torture a guy. I was so afraid I was going to slip inside you without any protection." He threw his arm over his eyes. "I tried not to come."

Her eyes rounded. She stared at him, stunned. "I…forgot."

"It's okay. I'm flattered you got so carried away."

He should be. She'd never been so irresponsible— so reckless. She exhaled, horrified with herself. The man was a dangerous distraction.

"We need to go inside and clean up, but I can't seem to move at the moment." He smiled lazily at her, his eyes warm and caring. Her heart melted. What she wouldn't do to have him always look at her that way.

But of course there was no always.

After today he would have no more interest in her. Her throat tightened. She rested her head against his chest.

If this was her gift—to always lose the man she

wanted—then she wasn't sure she wanted any part of it. She pushed aside the bleak picture of her future and focused on the steady beat of his heart beneath her ear. He was big and strong and incredibly sexy, but he wasn't hers. She had to remember that.

A hot breeze wafted over them. Dylan shifted and the hammock rocked. He ran his hand down her arm. "You're incredible. I haven't even been inside you yet, but somehow I feel so…fulfilled already."

Of course he did. Wasn't that the problem? And once she took him into her body, he'd be so fulfilled, he'd never want her again. Sadness billowed up inside her. This was no gift. It was a curse.

"Hey." He lifted her chin. "You're looking a little wrung out. I think I've let you wilt out here."

She forced a smile. "I'm okay."

Before she realized what he was doing, he swept her up and untangled them from the hammock. "You'll feel lots better after we clean you up. I've got a tub for two."

"There's a surprise. You like things big, don't you?"

He wiggled his eyebrows. "You should see my bed."

"Well…maybe after our bath…"

His smile split his face. What a difference from the other day. Where was the somber man who'd frowned so fiercely at her when Sebastian had climbed onto her shoulders?

"I like it when you smile," she said, tracing her finger along his lip.

"I haven't done much of that lately. Maybe it's time."

He hefted her more securely and headed toward a set of French doors that opened into the bedroom he apparently used for himself.

They moved past a king-size bed raised high on a platform, into the adjoining bathroom. It was roomy enough for the large garden tub that commanded its center, though not as big as the one off the master bedroom upstairs. Had he shared that room with the blonde in the picture, then moved downstairs to prevent being reminded of her?

Nikki shuddered. If that were the case, then it was a good thing they'd be making love here. The last thing she wanted was to compete with a lost love. Not that she was competing for anything. All she wanted was to help him over that loss.

He set her down on a soft gray rug. "Hey, you're supposed to be thinking only about me and my great body and what it can do for you." His eyes twinkled.

"So how do you know I wasn't?"

"You didn't have that sex-glazed look in your eye."

"My mind must have wandered. You'll have to remind me where we were."

He started the water running in the tub. With his gaze holding hers, he stripped off his shoes, loose shorts and briefs. He was magnificent. His broad shoulders and firm chest tapered into a narrow waist and hips. His muscles were well developed but not overly so.

His sex stirred as he closed the short distance between them. "That's better. Now you're looking hungry again."

She dipped her head. Her dress hung loosely around

her hips, disheveled and wrinkled. Warmth blossomed in her cheeks. "I'm a sight."

"That you are." He cupped her breast, thumbing her nipple. "This is the best you've looked so far. Not that you've ever looked bad. I just like you looking like you've had a good tumble."

"I don't think that counted as a tumble, technically speaking."

His eyebrows arched. "It was damn close."

She shrugged.

"You want to be tumbled?"

"It occurs to me that if you're going to tumble me, we should do that first. Otherwise we'll just need to clean up again."

"You do have a point. But how about a quick splash for now?"

"Okay."

"First you have to take this off." His fingers found the zipper at the back of her dress. The garment puddled around her ankles. She'd already lost her sandals somewhere in the shuffle.

He whistled softly. "Mmm-mmm, you look good enough to eat."

Taking her hand, he tugged her toward the tub. She stepped into the warm water after him. Following his lead, she sank to her knees, facing him. He turned off the water, then wet a fluffy washcloth.

"Promise you'll take a real bath with me later and I'll let you off easy this time."

"If you still want me to later, I will."

"Of course I'll want you to. Why wouldn't I want a beautiful naked woman in my tub?"

"Well, I'm here now." She grabbed a second wash-cloth and dunked it into the water, wringing it out slowly as he dabbed his cloth over her face, then down along her neck.

He wiped a path over her shoulders, then circled each breast, her nipples beading against the textured surface. Copying him, she swirled her cloth over his chest. He caught her mouth with his while he trailed down her abdomen, then lower, between her legs.

Matching each stroke of her tongue to a stroke of her hand, she wiped down his flat stomach, then ran the cloth over his erection, moaning softly as he circled her clitoris. His washcloth splashed into the water a second before he yanked hers from her hand.

Hastily he drew her to her feet, then pulled her toward his bedroom, grabbing two large towels along the way. "Time for your tumble."

She laughed as she wrapped the towel around her and climbed the steps to his massive bed. "You do like things big."

Grinning, he lifted her, then tossed her onto the mattress. "That's right. Don't you?"

Her gaze dropped to his burgeoning erection as he crawled up beside her. "Most definitely."

He kissed her again, taking his time, touching her tongue with long, slow strokes of his own. She savored the feel of his mouth on hers, his body hard and warm pressed against her, his fingers caressing her, sending that familiar heat spiraling through her. Slipping his hand between her legs, he broke the kiss.

"I like that you get so wet for me," he murmured as he caressed the swollen folds of her cleft.

She spread her knees wide and closed her eyes as he moved down her body, his fingers thrusting deep inside her, stretching her, readying her for their lovemaking. His lips brushed over each breast. He stopped to suckle her for a brief time, the pull of his mouth sending more heat flaring to her sex.

He kissed his way to her stomach, then down through her thatch of curls to her clit. Continuing the same lazy strokes, he circled his tongue over her for long moments while she moved against him, trying desperately to get him to increase his pace.

Then his tongue replaced his fingers inside her, thrusting into her with a delicious abandon. Fire licked through her, bringing her to a dizzying state of arousal. Softly she moaned his name.

He centered again on her clit, sucking her and laving her into a frenzied heat. She undulated against him, her breath hot and heavy. Light flashed behind her eyes and fire seared through her. He reached up and rolled her nipple between his fingers while his tongue circled her engorged flesh.

She cried out beneath him, this orgasm even more intense than the first. He slid up to hold her close. He stroked her back until her heart calmed enough for her to shift in his embrace. His erection pressed into her belly, yet he made no move to take her.

"You wonderful man," she whispered, then kissed him.

When she pulled back, her heart quickened at the heated look in his eyes. He was again the predator. And he had a fierce hunger to feed. She circled his erection with her fingers, then slowly drew her hand along his length.

"Make love to me, Dylan."

He closed his eyes and swallowed. "In the night-stand beside you."

Hurrying, she opened the drawer. She had to dig a bit but unearthed an assortment of condoms.

He rolled on one with a deft motion, then pinned her on her back, bringing his body over her. His erection pressed against her entrance. "Ah, Nikki, I don't deserve you."

"Yes, you do. We both deserve this." With a tilt of her hips she took him inside her.

Dylan groaned. She felt good. He dipped his head and kissed her as he moved, withdrawing, then easing back into her welcoming warmth. Heat ripped through him and he broke the kiss, raising up on his arms and tilting his pelvis to drive deeper into her.

Sounds of pleasure tore from her throat as she locked her legs around him and moved with him, urging him to a faster tempo. He held steady for an infinite time, lingering in that place on the brink of climax, then she cried out. Her muscles tightened around him, and his own release burst forward in a wild surge of fire and light.

He managed to shift to his side before collapsing. Nikki lay limp in his arms, the rapid rise and fall of her breasts mesmerizing him as his pulse thundered in his ears. He closed his eyes and drifted, willing his heartbeat to slow, a sense of incredible well-being filling him.

Nothing else existed beyond this room. For now, he lived in a fantasy world where this gorgeous creature looked at him with eyes that made him feel as if he was every woman's dream come true. She must be a dream. As a blissful lethargy pulled him into sleep, a vision swam through his mind.

A high wind buffeted angry waves all around him. Nikki, a seductive mermaid, held out her hand to him, beckoning him into the dark depths of the ocean.

5

"SAMSON IS SLEEPING AND Mrs. O'Brien has already picked up Pugsley. We still have the Andersons' poodle boarding and that cute little terrier. They're all fed and down for the night." Sarah plopped into the chair in front of Nikki's desk.

As young as Sarah was, fresh out of high school, she was a responsible and dedicated employee. Not only did she do all the grooming, she helped answer the phone and schedule appointments and she handled the clients with finesse and understanding. She also observed everything Nikki did with the same voracious curiosity Nikki had had at her age.

"Thanks, Sarah. Your mom on the way?"

The girl nodded. "I've almost got enough saved up for a car of my own, though. Can't wait to have my own wheels. I'll be heading off to room with some friends, who are looking for a third roommate. I just hate relying on my mom."

Nikki nodded. "I know the feeling. I got my driver's license the minute I turned sixteen, then moved out at eighteen."

Her chair squeaked as she leaned toward Sarah. "As much as we want our independence, we'll always have our families, though. We simply have to find a way to appreciate them."

"I appreciate my mom. I can just handle her better in small doses." A horn honked outside and Sarah rose reluctantly. "That's her. See you tomorrow."

Nikki bade her good-night, then turned to her list of calls. She'd like nothing better than to head home, but she was late checking on the pets she'd seen in surgery that day. For the next half hour she soothed owners' concerns and reinforced home care instructions.

"The coughing is normal. Her throat is a little sore from the anesthesia. It'll clear up in a couple of days. Just watch the incision to make sure there isn't any swelling, like we talked about. And please call if you have any more questions."

After a few more words of encouragement, Nikki hung up from her last call and glanced at the cat-shaped clock hanging on her office wall, the tail ticking away the minutes. The sun slanted low through the window. It had been a long day. Somehow she'd managed to concentrate on her work and not think about last night.

Last night. All her resolve to not think of Dylan melted as she laid her head on her arms and let memories of the previous evening flow over her. His mouth hot on hers, his tongue hungry and demanding. His hard body pressed on top of her, inside her. His look of amazement as they lay breathless afterward. He'd felt it, too—that incredible beauty and wonder over a joining that was meant to be.

She'd been intimate with her share of men, but it was as if all those times in the past had never happened. Her experience with Dylan eclipsed the rest. After he'd drifted to sleep, she'd stared at him a long moment, memorizing each curve of his restful face. Silently she'd kissed his cheek. Then she'd left, her heart heavy with the certainty that apart from the inspection and the closing, where they'd both be politely civil, she'd never see him again.

Her chest swelled with longing and her throat ached. Just the thought of him had her burning for his touch again. How was she supposed to move on? She didn't feel like embracing the world. She wanted to embrace Dylan, even if he never made love to her again. If only she could feel the strength of his arms around her one last time, making her feel safe and protected…and cherished as only he had made her feel.

She lifted her head and brushed moisture from her cheeks. "Buck up, McClellan. You knew the stakes going into this."

Still, the now too familiar melancholy gripped her as she hung her lab coat on the rack, grabbed her purse, then unlocked the front door to let herself out. The summer heat enveloped her immediately as she stepped off the front walkway onto the blacktop.

A number of cars dotted the lot of the shopping strip that housed her clinic. It took her a minute of squinting into the setting sun to find where she'd parked her battered Honda. She stopped.

A man leaned against her car, a dark silhouette against the brilliant red and orange hues. For a moment she tried to make out his features. He waved and her heart skipped a beat. Something in his bearing seemed very familiar.

Taking a deep breath, she moved forward, stifling the ray of hope that sprang up inside her. It couldn't be. Dylan was off conquering the world by now.

Yet the shape resembled him more and more with each step. Now the light gleamed off his blond hair and she could just make out the stormy blue of his eyes. She stopped in front of him, afraid to speak, afraid that if she so much as breathed he'd evaporate into the thick air.

"Working late?" he asked, his face impassive, guarded.

She nodded. Why was he there?

"I tried the door, but it was locked and no one answered when I knocked."

"Everyone else has gone home. I guess I didn't hear you."

A moment of silence followed. She shifted. The air hung hot and humid around them. Her cotton shirt clung to her back.

"I'm sorry I fell asleep last night," he said. "That doesn't usually happen."

"It's okay."

He nodded and jiggled his keys. "You were…incredible."

A knot formed in her throat. Heat seared her lungs. "I…um, I'm a little surprised to see you."

"You are? I hope it's okay that I stopped by." He shrugged, an easy shifting of his shoulders. "I had to see you again. I'm a little out of practice with this…dating thing. It's a big step for me, actually."

"Dating?"

"This—" he gestured back and forth between them "—relationship…" He stiffened, his eyes narrowing. "When you agreed to no-strings, you weren't thinking that was it?"

"What was it?" Her pulse beat in her ears.

"Last night. Nikki, you didn't just want a one-night stand, did you?"

A mixture of joy and unrelenting fear coursed through her. He still wanted her. But how would she withstand another encounter without losing herself to him completely? If it had been difficult to walk away from him last night, what would the next time be like?

"Nikki?"

"Are you saying you want more?"

"Hell, yes. Don't you?"

Yes. She wanted more. After just one night she wanted to take this as far as it would go—to see if what they had was real and if it was, then did it negate the curse? Would he stay with her in spite of her gift? *Could* he?

He blew out an impatient breath. "You promised me a bath."

"A bath?"

"You said if I still wanted to, you'd take a bath with me later. Well, it's later."

A slow smile spread across her lips. She did pride herself on keeping her word. "Yes, I did and I'm getting awfully sticky standing here in the heat."

"Then come home with me." He opened his arms and she stepped into his embrace, truly a one-night wonder no more.

DYLAN SHIFTED THE FOLLOWING morning, uncomfortable in his office chair. His second night with Nikki had been a night of wonders. So why did he feel like putting his fist through a wall?

"Have you got a minute?" Julie Foster asked as she hovered just inside his door. She brushed aside wispy blond bangs and bit her lip.

"Yes?" Dylan set down his pen and fought the urge to scowl at the woman. She was the third administrative assistant the practice had had in the past year and a half. The partners, let alone his father, would never forgive him if he ran off another one.

The last thing Dylan felt like doing right now was smiling, though. The night had been incredible and he'd done more than just smile. He'd laughed out loud. He'd groaned in ecstasy. He'd gone to heaven and back. Nikki certainly did wonders for his mood. Somehow the world seemed a brighter place when she was around. Leaving her snug in his bed so he could make it to work early had been torment, and now his normally sullen disposition had taken a turn for the worst.

Julie slipped farther inside the office and held out a sheaf of papers toward him. "These need your signature, then I'm to pass them on to your father for review...whenever you're through with them."

Dylan frowned as she dropped the stack on the corner of his desk. He could handle a prime case, but he still had to have all his paperwork checked? Would he ever win his old man's full approval?

She beat a hasty retreat to the door, wringing her hands. "And Councilman Weatherby is here for your ten o'clock."

"Damn." Frustration welled up inside him. He didn't have the patience for George Weatherby right now. The man expected Dylan to be grateful for the opportunity to represent him.

"You made this appointment last week and he's already in the reception area."

"It's not a problem." He blew out a breath and scrubbed his hands over his eyes. "Send him in. We might as well get this over with."

Steeling himself, he pasted on his best smile a few moments later as Julie ushered the man in, then hurried out, closing the door behind her. Dylan rose and extended his hand. "Councilman."

George Weatherby shook his hand, then mopped his

brow with a kerchief as he sank his bulk into the leather chair opposite Dylan's desk. "Hot as hell out there. I about melted just walking from my car to the door."

"Would you like something cold to drink?"

"I suppose a beer would be inappropriate?" The man slapped his knee and laughed as though he'd said something amusing. Dylan regarded him evenly until Weatherby straightened. "Actually some water would be really great."

After sending Julie for the requested beverage, Dylan settled again in his chair. He flipped through his file on the case. "Let's get on with the matter at hand. The court has ordered an evidentiary hearing for next week."

"Well, there isn't any evidence to hear! They won't find anything, because I didn't do anything." The man's expression darkened and his face flushed. "This is all Ted Johnson's doing. He hated that I beat him in the last election. I can tell you, I won't take this lying down. There will be hell to pay for maligning my name!"

"I understand you're upset by these charges. Fraud, extortion—either one would be cause for concern. But when we get to this upcoming hearing, it will be of utmost importance that you remain composed."

Weatherby's gaze narrowed. He leaned forward, the leather beneath him creaking in protest. "There's not going to be anything beyond this hearing, son. You hear me? Your daddy, for God knows what reason, has handed this case over to you, and I'm going along with him. Now you do your job and clear my name. You mess this up and I assure you this'll be the end of your career."

Dylan clenched his fists and inhaled deeply. Anger burned through him. "You can be assured I'll do my job, Councilman."

Julie knocked, then entered with the water. Weatherby swirled the drink, clinking the ice cubes against the glass. "Thank you, sweetheart. You're a lifesaver."

Pink tinged her cheeks. "Can I get you gentlemen anything else?"

Weatherby's gaze raked over the young woman in a way that twisted Dylan's gut. He gripped his pen. "That's all, Julie. Thank you."

She bobbed her head and scurried out the door. Weatherby smacked his lips, then took a long swallow. "That's better."

"About this evidentiary hearing—"

"It's nothing to worry about, my boy. Your old man briefed me over golf the other day."

"Did he?"

"They want to determine the facts of the case—get everyone's testimony and exhibit documents—which will all prove to be faked. Like I said, I'm innocent. The only way to prove otherwise is to forge the evidence. The witnesses will all be perjuring themselves. They'll be richer for it, I'm sure, but they'll be lying through their teeth."

"Lies are easy to unearth. If this thing goes to trial, we'll have the opportunity to cross-examine everyone.

Meanwhile, we'll be conducting interviews. I'll make a motion to suppress some of this evidence." Dylan waved at the folder. "The search warrant was questionable."

"It's all questionable."

"The community isn't feeling generous toward fraud these days. I want you to make me a list of character references and keep a diary of all significant occurrences and possible witnesses. You don't have any prior convictions. We'll do what we can to fight this."

"You do that, boy."

Clenching his fists to keep from throttling the man, Dylan rose. "We'll be in touch. Meanwhile, don't talk to anyone about the case, especially the press."

Slowly Weatherby heaved himself from the chair. "Well, guess I'll just go pop in to see that daddy of yours while I'm here."

"You do that…sir."

Weatherby narrowed his eyes, then a smile spread across his thick lips. "Maybe you'll manage this thing all right after all."

With one last backward glance he left. Dylan stared after him. Why the hell did he feel so compelled to remain in this practice? If he were the first Cain in generations to pursue a career outside of law, would that be such a bad thing?

DYLAN SLOWLY ROSE FROM THE bed where Nikki lay sleeping in the hours before dawn that Wednesday morning. A profound sense of peace such as he had not known in years spread over him. Being with her swept away all his work-related stress, making his life not only bearable but actually enjoyable. He showered, then dressed, and still she slept.

He glanced at the clock. It was early yet. The sun wouldn't rise for a couple more hours, but he was wide-awake, his body humming.

He had work to do, but instead he sank into the chair near the window, unable to take his gaze from her sleep-softened face. When was the last time he'd felt so alive? It seemed as though Nikki had roused a part of him he'd forgotten—or perhaps had never known.

At long last she stirred, rolling to her side and open-ing her eyes. Her lips curled into a slow smile that sent warmth flowing through him. He hadn't been able to re-sist calling her. He'd needed to see her. Somehow being with her drove away the darkness and made the present bearable. Any doubt he'd had in pursuing her had faded the moment she smiled at him.

Her smile transformed him.

She patted the bed beside her. "Why are you dressed and sitting way over there? Was I hogging the bed? Did I snore?"

"No." He moved from the chair to sit beside her and trace his finger along her smooth shoulder. She had the softest skin. "I don't sleep much."

"So talk to me. I want to know everything about you."

His stomach tightened. "There isn't anything to tell."

"Oh, I'll bet there is. Everyone has a story."

"You wouldn't be interested in mine."

Her expression softened. "Try me."

The gentle coaxing of her tone drew him closer, but he focused again on her skin as he ran his hand along her side, over the curve of her hip. She seemed so full of life and innocent to the seedier side of the world. He had to keep her safe from his personal life, where everything seemed so tainted.

"All that matters is the pleasure we give each other. The world doesn't exist outside this room, this time. When we're together, there is no past, no future. Only now," he said.

Her brow furrowed, but he bent to kiss her. The need to protect her surged through him. If he kept her here, in the safety of his home—his bed—he could keep her from harm. He had to make her understand that this incredible physical relationship was all they needed.

It was all he had to give.

"WHAT HAVE WE GOT TODAY?" Nikki scooped her hair into its usual ponytail as Sarah flipped through the schedule.

All that matters is the pleasure we give each other.

Taking a deep breath, Nikki squared her shoulders. She would not think of Dylan and whether or not she'd see him again. He'd been there that morning, watching her, waiting for her to wake. It had been more than she'd hoped for. Last night had been wonderful and she'd enjoyed each moment with him as if it were her last. Anything beyond this was the icing on the cake.

Her stomach tightened as she forced a smile. She would not worry. If she heard from him, then she'd value the time with him. If he didn't call…well, that would be that.

She'd survive.

A loose strand of hair brushed her cheek and she redid the ponytail. She should just cut her hair. Would Dylan like her better with a sleek, short style?

Sarah finally looked up. She popped a big pink gum-bubble, then sucked the wad back into her mouth. "Not too bad. Shots mostly."

"Okay, who's first?"

"The Harrises' cat, Lobo, that big Maine coon. They're in the waiting room."

"Nikki—" Janet, the receptionist, stuck her head in the door "—there's a call for you on line one. Sounds yummy."

"Oh, thanks. I'll take it in my office. Sarah, go ahead and take Lobo into room two and I'll be right there." Her heart sped as she hurried to her office, then shut the door. She lifted the receiver and punched the blinking button. "Hello?"

"Hi." Dylan's even baritone rumbled across the line.

She bit her lip to contain her smile—keep her hopes from soaring. She was losing it if something as simple as a phone call put her over the top like this. "Hi."

"You have completely sidetracked me with that luscious body of yours. I owe you a nice dinner."

"Oh." Her heart gave a squeeze. How she'd love to

go on a real date with him, but his reaction to her gentle probing this morning had proven to her more than ever that their relationship lived within strict boundaries.

He'd been right not to cross them.

"Nikki?"

"We agreed no frills."

Silence crackled across the line.

"It's okay. I knew what this was when I got into it," she said to reassure him.

"But I did ask you to dinner."

"That was before we made our deal."

"No frills."

"Right."

He was silent again.

She shifted. "I have to go. I have a patient waiting."

"Nikki."

"Yes?"

"Could I still see you tonight?"

She closed her eyes and let out a breath. "Yes."

"You'll come by when you get off?"

"I need to stop by my house, but I'll be there by eight."

"Eight o'clock it is." A light tone tinged his voice.

This time she let her smile burst forth. She'd been granted a reprieve. She'd see him again. She bade him goodbye, then hurried to see to her afternoon duties.

6

"WHERE WERE YOU LAST NIGHT?" Erin popped the top on a soda early that evening and frowned at Nikki. "Not that I mind having the apartment all to myself. Only two of Tess's minions stopped by, and they left early. I enjoy the privacy, but I don't like to worry. At least Tess always calls. You had your cell phone turned off."

Nikki shifted beside her youngest sister. "I'm sorry. I didn't mean to make you worry."

"I didn't worry until last night. Two nights in a row isn't like you, especially during the week. What was I supposed to think?"

"That I'd finally broken my record and actually found a man who wanted to stick around? Besides, I did come home early this morning to shower and change. You must have been sleeping like the dead not to have heard me."

Erin shrugged, her green eyes expressionless. "So have you?"

"Have I what?"

"Found a guy who's decided to stick around."

A vision of Dylan, his eyes full of desire, filled

Nikki's mind. She squelched the happiness blooming in her chest and affected a casual expression.

All that matters is the pleasure we give each other.

"Maybe," she said. "I'm seeing him again tonight. We'll see what happens after that. I'm taking it one day at a time with no expectations."

When we're together there is no past, no future. Only now.

"So who is he? Where did you meet him?"

"Actually I met him when I was out house hunting." She stopped to gauge her sister's reaction.

Erin's face remained impassive. "You've been house hunting? You're moving out of the apartment?"

"I've signed a contract on a place. I'm hoping you and Tess will move in with me."

Her sister made no comment, though her eyebrows arched slightly.

"Come on, Erin, a home of our own. Think about it. No landlords, no rent increases. But best of all, we won't ever have to move again."

"Have you mentioned this to Tess?"

"No, I haven't seen her. But she'll be thrilled."

"Maybe. As long as she can have her minions over, she'll be happy wherever."

"I do think I understand her a little better now."

"What's to understand? She sleeps around. She keeps a dozen or so poor slovenly fools at her beck and call at any one time." Her gaze met Nikki's. "She's just like our mother."

"I don't think it's quite like that. Sophie explained some of it to me. Maybe we should sit down." She grabbed a bottle of wine and two glasses.

Erin shook her head and plopped down at one of the kitchen chairs. "Why is it I get the feeling that I am not going to like this?"

"You probably won't. I'm not so sure about it myself." She served them both, then took a long swallow before continuing. "You know that show where the three sisters grew up to discover they were witches?"

"Yeah. What's that got to do with anything?"

"Well, that's kind of us, only we're not witches—at least I don't think so. I need to verify with Sophie. She does brew up her little potions—"

"What are you talking about?"

"I went to see Sophie after Brad dumped me…you know, after we finally— Anyway, I was upset that I couldn't seem to keep a man until morning."

"And?"

"And she had an unusual explanation." She paused. How could she ease Erin into this?

"Which was?"

"Well, she said the women in our family all share a gift and apparently it manifests a little differently in each of us." She took a breath and faced her sister. "We have the gift of sexual healing."

Erin laughed. "Sexual healing? You have got to be kidding me."

"I know it sounds ridiculous, but I'm thinking there might be something to this."

"You mean healing men by having sex with them?"

Nikki nodded. "It does sound unbelievable. Believe me, I know."

"And we're *all* supposed to have this gift?"

"Right, according to Sophie."

"Well, that *is* ridiculous. I can guarantee I don't have any such gift."

"How can you be so sure? I never see the guys I sleep with again. For all I know, they really are out conquering the world."

Erin pushed her glass away. "Nikki, you can't believe this."

A vision of Dylan came to Nikki. Peace softened his expression and calmed the turbulence of his psyche. "I don't know. Maybe."

"And you think this excuses Maggie's and Tess's behavior?"

"I think it's a possible explanation."

"If you say so." Erin stood, her mouth quirked in a half smile. "Sounds like foolishness to me."

"Just consider it for a moment. What if it *is* true? Is it such a bad thing?"

"You are losing it. Look, I've got some errands to run." With a shake of her head Erin strode from the room.

Nikki stared after her. Maybe she hadn't expected her sister to accept Sophie's theory off the bat, but she hadn't expected her to completely discount it, either.

Somehow it had made Erin…nervous. What would make her have such an odd reaction?

NIKKI PUSHED ASIDE HER worries over her sister as she stood on Dylan's doorstep later that evening. Her stomach clenched with a combination of anticipation and dread. What if he'd been angered by her refusal to go to dinner? What if he'd finally been struck with the need to run off and conquer the world?

Only one way to find out. She pressed the doorbell.

It seemed odd that in a few short weeks this would be her doorbell, her house. Her heart lightened as footsteps sounded from inside.

She tamped down on the joy bubbling in her, but when Dylan stood before her it seemed the floodgates opened. All her relief and happiness spilled out and she was unable to form a coherent thought.

He stared at her for the briefest heartbeat, then his hand cupped the back of her head and tugged her to him. His mouth covered hers, his lips parting and his tongue seeking, probing.

She wrapped her arms around him and melted into the kiss, savoring the heat of it, the excitement emanating from him. He wanted her.

He broke the kiss, resting his forehead against hers. "Hi."

"Hi."

"Want to come in?"

"Sure."

He took her hand and led her straight into his bed-room, nodding toward a table laden with delicious smelling take-out boxes. "I ordered Chinese. It's not quite the dinner I envisioned when I called this after-noon, but I hope that's okay."

A twinge of disappointment stung her. It would have been nice to let him take her out on a real date, but she shook off the thought. They'd made a deal. And it was very sweet of him to provide a meal. "Sure. Chinese is fine. It smells heavenly."

He pulled her close again. "You're okay with stay-ing in? I know we agreed no frills—"

"I am absolutely okay with staying in." She let her gaze wander over him. He seemed to look better each time she saw him. No, staying in definitely wouldn't be a problem.

"Good, I really didn't feel like going back out. Be-sides…" he ran his hand up her arm "…I like the idea of having you all to myself—my secret indulgence."

She smiled. "I like it with just the two of us, too. I'm all for secret indulgences."

"Perfect. That's the way we'll keep it."

She leaned over and sniffed the closest container. "Is that sweet-and-sour shrimp?"

"Uh-huh." He nuzzled her neck while he cupped her bottom. "But maybe we should skip to dessert."

"Here, sit." She gently pushed him into one of the chairs, lifted shrimp and a pair of chopsticks, then strad-dled his lap. "Maybe we can combine the two."

His eyes lit with excitement. "Sounds like my kind of meal."

She gripped a fat shrimp with the chopsticks, then dangled the morsel over his lips. He smiled and seated her more securely in his lap, anchoring her by her hips. "No teasing."

"No teasing." She lowered the shrimp and he bit it into his mouth.

"Mmm." His eyes closed as he savored the bite. Then he fed her a shrimp from his fingertips.

The sweet-and-sour flavor rolled over her tongue as she chewed slowly, her gaze never leaving his. She'd barely swallowed before he pulled her into another breathtaking kiss. The heat of his mouth—of his desire—rolled over her as she savored the feel of his tongue on hers.

When he stood, she wrapped her legs around him, clinging to him as he carried her to the bed. His mouth never left hers as he settled on the mattress with her. For long moments she lost herself in the kiss, in the hungry wandering of his hands over her back, breasts and buttocks. He caressed her through her clothes and she touched him in like, her fingers tracing the curve of his shoulder, the cut of his biceps and his chest, hard beneath the soft cotton shirt.

"I need to touch you." She tugged his shirt over his head, feasting her gaze on the muscled contours of his torso.

His eyes closed as she stroked her hand over him.

Warmth swirled in the pit of her stomach. *Pleasure.* Touching him gave her so much pleasure. She brushed her lips over him, trailing kisses to his male nipple. He moaned and threaded his fingers in her hair as she laved him. He let her have her way with him for several long moments.

Then he growled softly and rolled her to her back. "I need to touch you, too…everywhere."

He peeled her clothes from her with sure movements, his gaze tracing each exposed inch of her. He sat back. "Let me look at you."

She lay still, his need lifting hers, sending that ache deep inside her until she pulsed with it. "Touch me, Dylan."

Something dark and intense flashed through his eyes. He reached out to cup her breast with a tenderness that nearly brought tears to her eyes. He lowered his head and kissed her nipple, brushing his lips lightly over her until her flesh beaded. He took her into his mouth and she cried out as the heat arrowed through her.

Her sex swelled and moistened. She tugged at his waistband. He moved away long enough to rid himself of the rest of his clothes.

"Hurry," she urged as he rolled on a condom.

His lips quirked in a half smile as he seated himself deep inside her. He held her gaze for a long moment before he moved, and when he did, her cry of pleasure matched his.

She couldn't tell if this incredible joy was his or hers

or something combined that existed only in this moment of joining.

His image blurred and she blinked uncalled-for tears from her eyes. The tenderness in his gaze brought an ache to her throat. He kissed her, a light touch of his lips to hers, as he thrust again and she came, the orgasm rippling out and gripping him in its power, so that he cried out and joined her.

"HUNGRY?" NIKKI'S SISTER, Tess, called from the kitchen as Nikki straggled into the apartment late that night. She tiptoed past Clark, another of her sister's past loves, who lay snoring on the living room sofa, to step into the well-lit kitchen.

Tess wore an apron over a nightie. She hefted a wooden spoon as her current boyfriend, Ramon, dressed in a pair of low-riding shorts, stirred something in a big pot on the stove. He snaked his arm around Tess and pulled her in for a quick kiss. The scent of garlic permeated the air.

Nikki's stomach tightened at the easy affection. Even though the brief dinner with Dylan had been most exciting and their after-dinner romp had been even more satisfactory, she hadn't been able to shake the feeling of gloom that had settled over her as he'd drifted to sleep beside her. The incredible high of their lovemaking had been too fleeting.

She could have stayed with him through the night as she was in the habit of doing. They probably would have enjoyed another tumble or two during the night.

But as his arm had grown heavy across her waist and his breathing had leveled into the steady rhythm of sleep, the urge to flee had gripped her.

And even though she'd eaten very little of their dinner, her appetite for once eluded her.

"No, thanks." She squinted at the kitchen clock. "It's after one in the morning and you two are cooking?"

"This one has sapped me. A man needs to keep his strength up." Ramon ran a possessive hand over Tess's hip.

She laughed and snuggled in closer to him. "Ramon is taking me to meet his family tomorrow and he insists we bring them food that I helped prepare so I can win them over."

"They'd love her no matter what," he said. "Why wouldn't they? I can't get enough of her."

"Of course you can't, but could I just borrow her for a minute?" Nikki asked.

Both Ramon and Tess turned to her, eyebrows raised in question.

"I won't keep her long. It's late and I have to work in the morning."

"Sure." Tess extricated herself, giving him a quick kiss on the cheek. "Don't let your sauces cool."

"Mmm, you keep me hot. Don't keep me waiting too long, or I'll come after you."

Nikki rolled her eyes and dragged her sister down the hall to her bedroom. She plopped on her bed, and Tess sank into the big cushioned chair that had been Nikki's first furniture purchase when she'd gotten the apartment.

It was wide and deep with cushions a body could get lost in. It had taken two of Tess's bulkiest minions to move it into the room. To Nikki it represented permanence. She'd always have this chair and she meant to always have a home in which to house it.

"So you've got a new guy?" Tess tossed her mass of red waves, her crystal-blue eyes round with curiosity.

Not for the first time, Nikki marveled at how much her sister favored Maggie. She and Erin both had their respective fathers' coloring. Tess had their mother's fiery looks and carefree attitude.

"That's not what I want to talk about."

"No?"

"No." She shifted on the bed, hugging a pillow with a ruffled trim to her front. "I went over this with Erin earlier and it didn't go too well."

"What's with her?"

"She's been a little…moody lately."

"Moody? That's a nice way of putting it. I walk into the room and she leaves like I'm stinking up the place."

"I think part of it might be that she values her privacy."

"I'm hardly ever here. She gets plenty of privacy."

"But, Tess, your minions are always around, whether you're here or not."

Tess rolled her eyes. "I don't ask them to do things for me. They just do. I didn't hear her complaining when Alex came over to fix the garbage disposal or Ben brought in all those live plants or Jeffrey steam-cleaned the furniture and carpets."

"No, but maybe it bothers her to see you crook your little finger and a dozen guys come running."

"If she ever gave any of them half a chance, she'd get the same reaction."

"Perhaps." Nikki squished the pillow down and sat straighter. "I had this talk with Sophie the other day. It was…illuminating."

"Sophie's talks are always illuminating."

"Well, this one was more so. It was about the women of our family…about us."

Tess cocked her head in question, her face taking on the exact same expression their mother's did when she focused on something that interested her.

Nikki inhaled, then blew out her breath. She could just say this to Tess. She would understand. "We're sexual healers."

Her sister's eyes rounded in a moment of surprise, then her lips curled into a slow smile. "Sure, that makes sense."

Just like that. Total acceptance.

Nikki shook her head. "Somehow I knew you'd be okay with it."

"Well, why not?" Her smile brightened to show straight white teeth. "We're like the Halliwell sisters, only… Hey, are we witches?"

"No! At least I don't think so. Wouldn't that throw Erin into a tizzy?"

"So our baby sister didn't go for the sexual-healing thing?"

"Not really. I think it…I don't know…disturbed her? I haven't had a chance to talk to her more."

"I'll handle it."

"Maybe you should let me do that."

Tess shrugged. "So all of us? All the women of our family? Like Maggie? Aunt Sophie?"

"All the women."

"We heal men by loving them."

"That's the word."

"You know, that explains why I fall in love with every single one of them."

"You do?"

"Oh, yes, with all my heart. Don't you?"

Nikki sank back against the headboard. Did she fall in love each time? She thought about her former lovers, and with each image her chest filled with warmth until her heart seemed to expand and the warm feeling flowed over her. At the memory of Dylan sleeping, his face softened with peace, the warmth expanded, blurring the room. "Maybe so."

"Exactly. Why didn't I figure this out sooner? Let's call Sophie." Tess reached for the phone on Nikki's nightstand.

"It's nearly two in the morning."

"You don't think she'll be up?"

"No."

"Guess if she is, she might not be alone. Wouldn't want to interrupt anything," Tess said.

"Sophie?"

"Well, yeah. She's got the gift, right?"

"Theoretically."

"So don't you think she uses it?"

"I don't want to think about that," Nikki said.

"Hey, those old geezers need healing, too."

"Sophie's not old."

"She wears her age well, just like Maggie. Sure she's not a witch?"

"This conversation is getting a little out of control."

"It's all straight. I thought you were loosening up." Tess reached over and thumped Nikki on the arm. "So you using your gift on your new guy?"

"I'm not sure how I feel about this…this gift."

"What's there to feel? It is, so you accept it." She hopped up suddenly. "Speaking of which, I've got a hungry man waiting for me."

"Wait…there's something else I need to tell you about."

Tess perched on the edge of the bed, her body tense. Her mind had already shifted gears and she was obviously anxious to be off.

Nikki tossed the pillow aside. Truth time. She hadn't stopped to think how her sister would respond to her news about the house.

Her heart thudded. Tess might take this as an opportunity to run off with her lovers, the way Maggie had done. The prospect disheartened her. As crazy as Tess could be, life just wouldn't be the same without her.

"I'm buying a house," Nikki said.

Tess nodded. "Cool. I know you've wanted that for a while. Good for you."

"Thanks. I'm hoping you and Erin will move in with me. It's got plenty of room. We'd have lots of privacy. And there's this courtyard area… Well, it's really nice." She paused, unsure of what else to say. "So maybe you could go see it with me sometime."

"Of course I'd like to see it."

"Great. I'll arrange it. Maybe we can get Erin to come with us, too." The thought of showing her sisters the house didn't unnerve Nikki nearly as much as the thought of introducing them to Dylan. Maybe they could see it while he was at work.

"Okay, just let me know what works with your schedule. I'm not anchored to the nursery these days. Maybe we can go tomorrow afternoon. Isn't that your half day at the clinic?"

"I'll call my agent in the morning."

Tess turned in the door. "I do want to hear about this guy sometime."

"Sure. Soon."

Talking to her sisters about Dylan somehow seemed an infringement on her deal with him. Maybe later, when her time with him had ended, she'd tell Tess and Erin about him…and find a way to heal herself.

7

THE SKIES OPENED THE NEXT morning, pouring down rain, soaking the earth and relieving some of the ever-present humidity. Dylan frowned out his office window, damning the gray day for no particular reason. He'd gone to sleep with an angel in his arms, then awakened alone, his air conditioner blasting, fogging the windows and doors, chilling him to the bone. He'd reached for his phone to call her to demand she return to warm his bed, bringing her beautiful face and body over to distract him from the demons. But he'd stopped mid-dial.

He shouldn't need her like this.

He closed his eyes. He hated the rain. Memories of that night two years ago descended on him—the screeching tires, the horrific boom of the car as it collided with the pole, his heart pounding in the subsequent stillness before the power lines fell in a fury of fire.

He squeezed his eyes closed against the memory, as if he could blot out the events that had followed. The heaviness shrouded him, choked him. He reached for the phone. If he could just hear Nikki's voice. She could reach across the line and touch him—connect with him—bestowing her soothing magic on him. What kind of woman was she that just the hint of a smile from her brightened his day beyond reason and loving her…

The phone rang as he gripped the handset. Swallowing hard, he whipped the receiver from its cradle. "Cain here."

"Dylan, it's Ginger Parker. Did I catch you at a good time?"

"Sure, Ginger, what can I do for you?"

"Ms. McClellan would like to see the house again. She wants to show it to her sisters."

His stomach tightened. So Nikki had sisters. He fisted his hand around a pen and stabbed the point into a legal pad. A morass of emotions gripped him: relief that she'd scheduled through the real-estate agent, keeping him out of her family loop and a loss over what to do with this bit of personal information. It didn't fit into the tidy definition he'd scribed for her in his life.

"Dylan?"

"Yes, that's fine. When?"

"Would early afternoon, around twelve-thirty today, work?"

"Sure. The lockbox is still on," Dylan said.

"Very good. I'll let her know."

"Please be sure not to let the cat out."

"Of course. Have a good day and please don't hesitate to let me know if you need anything."

"Right. Thanks, Ginger." He hung up and stared again out the window.

She had sisters. And what of her other family—aunts, uncles…parents?

"No." He shook his head to banish the questions.

He didn't want to know about her. He had no right, not when he couldn't reciprocate. She was better off away from his family—from any of the personal dealings of his life. He'd let Kathy in and what had it gotten her?

Dead. It had killed her. He'd be damned if he would let that happen again. And all he had left to show for it was that big empty house. Good riddance. Nikki and her sisters were welcome to it.

"OH MY GOD." TESS STOPPED in the bright entryway, her gaze sweeping the stained glass above the door. The rain had stopped and sunlight poured through the jewel-colored panes. "This isn't a house. It's more like an estate."

"It isn't that big." Nikki shook her head and stooped to pet Sebastian, who ran lazy eights around her legs.

At least one of her sisters seemed adequately impressed. She couldn't shake the disappointment that Erin had opted not to come. Her youngest sibling seemed more and more inclined to keep to herself. Maybe telling her about the whole sexual-healing theory had been a mistake.

"Hey, where's *my* room?" As always, Tess cut to the chase.

Without waiting for Nikki or Ginger, she raced up the curved stairway toward the second floor. "Do I have my own bathroom? Is there a view of the gardens?"

As Nikki followed Ginger up the stairs, she had to smile at Tess's childlike exuberance. "All the rooms overlook the gardens."

They caught up with Tess in the master bedroom. Nikki sobered immediately. She'd forgotten about this room. She and Dylan spent all of their time in the downstairs bedroom. She hadn't been in here since her initial tour of the house.

Heavy curtains covered the floor-to-ceiling windows, casting deep shadows throughout the room. Framed pictures of Dylan and the beautiful blonde dotted one nightstand and the dresser, where a goldbacked brush and mirror resided beside an ornate jewelry box.

Her jewelry box. A deep melancholy swamped Nikki as she stood staring at the image of a mermaid inlaid in colorful stones along the box's lid. Had he also commissioned this piece for the mysterious woman?

"Ugh, you can have this room." Tess wrinkled her nose as Ginger pulled open the drapes.

Before either Ginger or Nikki could comment, Tess raced out of the room to explore the rest of the floor. Her cry of delight greeted them as they entered the hall.

She poked her head out of a door a few feet away and waved them on. "This is the one. I claim it. Old Erin, sourpuss, can take the leftovers. Look at how the light plays over the walls."

The light did seem to shimmer along the walls and ceiling in a way Nikki hadn't noticed in the other rooms.

"They used some kind of finish like a pickling," Ginger said. "I've seen it in furniture but never on a wall. It's very nice. I hadn't noticed it before. It must be the way the light is slanting through the window."

Nikki smiled and grinned at Ginger as Tess went on to plan where each piece of her furniture would fit. "And look at the closet! I think it might actually fit all my shoes," she said, clapping her hands in delight.

For just a moment Nikki let herself get caught up in Tess's enthusiasm. Thank God Tess wasn't getting Maggie's wanderlust. Buying the house had been the right decision for Nikki and her sisters. They'd be happy here. And Erin would come around. As much as Tess teased her, the two had always gotten along. Tess would talk to her, to get her excited about the move.

"You know, Peter Houston's brother is a mover. Just bought a huge van. I'll see what their schedule's like. When are we moving?" Tess turned to her, eyebrows raised in expectation.

"In about four weeks. We can schedule them, but nothing's final until we close." Nikki grinned. With Tess's long line of exes at their disposal, they never lacked for any service they might require.

"Oh, you'll close all right. Mr. Cain is most anxious to tie this up," Ginger said.

"Is he?" For some inexplicable reason Nikki's stomach tightened.

"Yes, says he's ready to move on with his life. I've never seen a man more determined." Ginger cocked her

head thoughtfully. "I've a feeling he will see this
through come hell or high water."

Come hell or high water. A chill passed through
Nikki when they again neared the master bedroom.
What haunted past drove Dylan? What made him so determined to move away? Surely his departure from this
house would signal his departure from her life.

If he was still around by then.

Maybe the question was, would she be able to exor-
cise the ghosts once she and her sisters had moved in
and Dylan had left to conquer the world?

"SO YOU BROUGHT YOUR SISTERS to see the house." Dylan
leaned against the massive headboard, light from the
bedside table falling across his chest and shoulders.

"One of them." Nikki shrugged, trying not to make
too much of the fact that this was the first time they'd dis-
cussed anything remotely personal. "She liked it a lot."

He nodded and she settled beside him on his bed, her
excitement at being with him barely contained. "I
wasn't sure you'd call me again."

"To be honest, I tried really hard not to." He slid his
hand up her thigh.

"Really?"

His eyes fixed on hers and the need, the desire, emanating from him was so real, it took her breath away.
Her mood lightened. He may fight it, but he wanted her.

His voice was low, his gaze troubled, when he continued. "I shouldn't need you like this."

"It's okay." She brushed her lips over his. "I need you, too."

He crushed her to him then, taking her mouth with that hunger that made her knees weak, rolling with her so his body covered hers, pressing her into the softness of the bed. His tongue dueled with hers while his hands explored her through her clothes. He stroked her hips, her thighs and her belly.

He broke the kiss to nuzzle her neck, his warm breath sending ripples of pleasure through her as he freed the buttons of her shirt. He kissed a path along her collarbone.

"Touch me, Nikki."

She slipped her hands under his shirt, caressing the broad planes of his chest, the firm muscle and his taut nipples. He broke away to whip the shirt over his head, then covered her again. It seemed he touched her everywhere at once. She shivered as he swept off her shirt and bra in one quick motion.

"Warm me," she whispered.

He blew on her breast, then took her in his mouth, teasing her nipple until her heart quickened and heat spread through her veins. She stroked his back, his shoulders, then delved her fingers into his thick hair as he suckled first one breast, then the next.

"Oh, Dylan…" She moaned softly and lost herself in the strong pull of his mouth.

Then his hands were at her waistband. He stripped the rest of her clothes from her and she lay naked before him. The light in his eyes, the appreciation, sent a thrill of satisfaction running through her. A sense of power rose in her. Was this how she'd made the others feel?

But he kissed her again, filling her thoughts, her senses. She breathed deeply of his scent—so clean and strong and uniquely Dylan. She pulled it into her lungs and committed to memory the feel of him, the light playing off his smooth skin and his soft growl of arousal as she pushed his pants over his hips.

She helped him out of his clothes, then she touched him. His skin was smooth, sensitized to her touch so it seemed by the ripples of excitement that flowed from him. She caressed his arms, his chest and the flat plane of his stomach. He groaned and rolled to his side as she stroked her hand up his thigh to his erection. He was thick and hard and so hot. Her own sex pulsed with the need to take him inside her.

His fingers found her wet and ready. She circled him with her hand and matched her stroke to his as he readied her for their loving. Shivers of arousal shimmered over her. "Dylan, I can't wait."

He nodded, then kissed her quickly. She tried to steady her breath as he rolled on a condom, then spooned her from behind, pulling her hips close and running his hand up her inner thigh to her clit. Her heart raced as his erection pressed into her.

"Like this?" he asked.

"Yes."

His fingers strummed her as he thrust into her and she cried out with the pleasure. "Yes, Dylan…"

He spoke her name with what seemed a note of reverence that touched her more deeply than any caress. She was swept away in his rhythm as he stroked in and out with both strength and gentleness at once, never neglecting her pleasure as his fingers worked their magic over her swollen flesh. The tension coiled around her in waves of intense pleasure. Electricity prickled along her spine, then seemed to bloom outward as the first ripples of orgasm hit her.

She covered his hand with hers and squeezed as light exploded behind her eyes and she cried out. He thrust once, twice as the shock of release left her limp in his arms. He groaned and held her tight, burying his face in the crook of her neck.

DYLAN STARTLED AWAKE. Disoriented, he pushed himself upright. Moonlight streamed through an opening in the curtain and pooled on the floor. His heart pounded and a feeling of doom pressed down on him. Something was terribly wrong. He closed his eyes and tried to focus on the wretchedness gripping him.

He'd been dreaming about Kathy. He reached through his consciousness for her, but the dream slipped away, dissipating like fog. Her essence lingered, as though she'd just walked through the room and would return at any moment. But he knew that she would not.

Kathy was gone.

The agony hit him like a knife to his gut, bending him over, knocking the breath from him. He crouched on the side of the bed, his arms on his knees, as despair swallowed him.

How long he sat that way, fighting the demons, he couldn't tell. But after a time, the stillness of the room crept over him. The stillness and the steady breathing of the woman who slept beside him...

Nikki.

Just the thought of her brought a respite from the blackness. She had come to mean so much to him in so short a time. For a moment he stared at her, almost surprised to find her there, though the memory of their earlier encounter flowed readily through his mind.

Filling him with guilt.

He'd been weak to call her again. How could he have betrayed Kathy's memory this way? He hadn't meant for his relationship with Nikki to become anything more than what they'd agreed on—an expression of the simple pleasure between a man and a woman. But somewhere along the way he'd lost sight of that intention. Somewhere along the way he'd started to care about her.

Anger and guilt warred in him, driving him from the warmth of his own bed. He tried desperately to picture Kathy's face, but the image eluded him. He paced in the darkness, feeling suddenly caged and wanting to lash out at...what, he didn't know. But this was wrong.

He shouldn't be here with Nikki while Kathy lay cold in the ground. It wasn't fair to Kathy's memory. And it wasn't fair to Nikki that he couldn't give her more of himself. She may have insisted that she was content to keep their relationship confined to the bedroom, but at times her eyes told a different story. He'd seen the longing for more there, though he'd refused to recognize it.

He plucked his jeans off the back of a chair and dressed. He needed air. He couldn't be here anymore. He needed to clear his head so he could prepare for that hearing Monday morning. With one last glance at the soft form in the bed, he grabbed his keys, then left.

A FAR-OFF KNOCKING DRAGGED Nikki from a place between sleep and consciousness—a place where whispers of truth both nagged and teased her. She opened her eyes to bright sunlight streaming through the curtains. Frowning, she pushed aside the thick comforter, then plopped back as memories of her night with Dylan flooded back to her. She'd returned to her office after showing Tess the house to find that he'd called.

The knocking sounded again, followed almost immediately by the chime of the doorbell. She didn't have to reach across the bed to feel his absence. It weighed down on her like an oppressing chill she might never shake.

He was gone.

For a moment she lay not breathing, an imaginary vise clamping her chest. Her throat burned and the room blurred. She'd known this moment would come, but damn it, did it have to hurt so much?

The pounding came again, louder and more insistent.

"Damn it." She tossed the blankets aside, then dragged on the first thing she saw—Dylan's bathrobe.

As she stormed toward the door, she let her upset simmer into a good anger—not that she could quite blame Dylan for a response that was most likely beyond his control, but she could rail at whatever higher power that had "gifted" her with this healing curse.

She yanked open the door. "Yes?"

A beautiful blonde blinked at her. For just an instant Nikki thought it was the woman in the many photos around the house. But it couldn't be. This woman lacked the warmth of the one in the pictures. In fact, a feeling of superiority emanated from the woman at the door, something that seemed foreign to the photographed blonde.

The hair on the back of Nikki's neck bristled. What business did this woman have with Dylan?

The stranger's gaze raked Nikki from head to toe, then back again, her eyes widening, then narrowing in speculation. "Who are you?"

"I'm the one wearing the robe. Who the hell are you?" Her conscience prickled. This was no way to speak to Dylan's visitor, but the blonde rubbed her the wrong way.

The woman straightened, raising her chin and puffing out her chest like some offended hen. "I'm Evelyn Rogers. I'm a friend of Dylan's. I've known his family for years."

All the fight drained out of Nikki. Her own insecurities flooded her, temporarily obscuring any sense she might have of Evelyn. Nikki pulled the robe tighter around her, feeling like an imposter. Or worse. "Right. Of course you have."

"So I take it Dylan isn't here."

"It doesn't appear so."

"I also work with him. I brought him this." She pulled a file from her briefcase. "He said he'd want it to work on over the weekend."

Nikki took the file from her, staring at it a moment. So Evelyn knew Dylan personally as well as professionally. Her gloom deepened. She knew so little of him. She tamped down on the envy flooding her. "It's for a case he's working on—the one with the councilman—isn't it?"

"Those records are confidential."

Heat filled Nikki's cheeks. "Of course. I'm sure it's all legalese anyway."

"It is." A stronger wave of superiority flowed off Evelyn. "It isn't the councilman who interests you, is it?" Her gaze dropped to the file. "You're dying to know more about Dylan."

"I'm slightly curious is all. He…doesn't speak much of his work."

"No, I'm sure the two of you have more interesting things to…discuss."

Nikki nodded, her lips pressed together. Even without her sixth sense, she couldn't miss the woman's jealous tone. Evelyn Rogers might call herself Dylan's friend, but she wanted much more from him than his friendship. Nikki's gaze fell to the magnificent diamond on Evelyn's ring finger and she felt empathy for the man who'd put it there.

She gripped the folder. "I'll make sure he gets this."

"Thank you." Evelyn started to turn away, then stopped. "This is absolutely none of my business, but you're the first, you know."

Nikki's empathic nature resurfaced. A strong curiosity replaced the woman's earlier holier-than-thou vibe. "The first?"

"The first woman he's had here since the accident."

Nikki nodded. *The accident.* So there *had* been one. Never in a million years would she admit to this woman she knew nothing of Dylan's life. "I thought that might be the case."

"Well…I'm happy to see he seems to be coming out of it."

She spoke the truth. On some level she did seem to care about Dylan. "So you're close?"

"Sure. I've known him for years. I'm like an adopted daughter to his parents."

"I see. You and he are like brother and sister then."

Evelyn stiffened. "I suppose you could look at it that way. Of course, I'm with Nick, and Dylan… Well, don't be disappointed if he never quite gets over his first love."

"Of course. He loved her." Bitterness tinged her words.

Evelyn's eyes took on a sympathetic light. "I'm guessing like no man has ever loved a woman before or since."

"Right. Certainly. I'm sure they were a lovely couple."

"Could I offer some advice?"

Nikki cocked her head. No way was she trusting this woman. "Why not?"

"He obviously saw something in you or you wouldn't be here. Kathy was…special. You're better off making a new place for yourself in his life, if you're able. My guess is he's closed off a big part of himself since her death. Leave it alone and be happy with whatever he has left to offer." She shrugged. "Maybe in time that little bit will grow."

Nikki nodded. As genuine as Evelyn seemed at the moment, she had ulterior motives. "Yes, thanks…Evelyn." She offered the blonde her hand. "I'm Nikki McClellan."

"Nikki." She squeezed her fingertips. "It's a pleasure, I assure you."

Nikki managed a tight smile as she bade Evelyn farewell and shut the door. Her head swam with the new information. Dylan's lost love's name had been Kathy. She'd died. And he'd loved her as no man had ever loved a woman before or since.

Great. It was worse than she thought. And now she had this *friend* of Dylan's to contend with. This was turning out to be quite a morning. And damn it, she was late for work.

8

"TESS IS ALL OVER IT, BUT Erin…" Nikki shook her head. It was Sunday afternoon and Nikki found herself at Sophie's again.

Sophie poured them both more tea from an antique teapot she claimed had been in the family for generations, passed on from some Louisiana cousins. "She's not ready to hear about her heritage. Don't push her. She'll come round in her own time."

"I just want her to be happy with everything. She hasn't been herself lately."

"We each have our own path to walk. You must allow her free rein of hers."

"I suppose. I really hoped both she and Tess would be excited at the prospect of settling down permanently somewhere."

"Nikki, darling, don't be distressed if they have their own dreams to follow."

"But how could they not want to settle down?"

Sophie gave her a knowing look.

"Okay, I can see where Tess might be happy to flit around like Maggie did, though unlike our mother,

Tess has always kept a base with us. I just don't understand Erin."

"Give her some time. She's not quite ripe yet."

Leave it to Sophie to equate Erin with fruit.

Sophie laid her hand on Nikki's. "Want to talk about why you're really here?"

"I'm sure you can guess." Her throat tightened and she gritted her teeth. She would not cry.

"It was time for your bird to fly?"

"Why was this one so different?"

"You were with him longer?"

She laughed a short, raspy laugh. "This one lasted about a week. A real record breaker."

Sophie's eyebrows arched. "Interesting."

"Did he just need that much more healing?"

"Could be."

"He lost someone." Those damn tears threatened. "Her name was Kathy. He loved her more than any man has ever loved a woman before or since. She died in some accident."

"Yes, a wound of the heart. Very tricky, those. Did he open up, let it all out?"

"Open up? You mean, did he ever talk to me about being so unhappy?"

"Talking acts as a release. When you have a boil that's infected, the infection has to be released. This is the same. If he hasn't spoken of it, the injury has likely festered."

"We never talked much. He avoided any conversations about his personal life. I never pressed him."

Sophie shook her head. "There is something about the gift that coaxes the healing. I'd think after a week with you, he'd have spilled it all. My guess is if he hasn't opened to you, he hasn't opened to anyone."

"But he's gone. I woke up Friday morning and he had left already. I didn't hear from him and I don't think he'll call again. This time was…different. It felt more final."

"And this hurts?"

The pain in Nikki's throat grew unbearable. She nodded and closed her eyes as tears spilled down her cheeks. "Why? Why is it so hard for me when Maggie and Tess breeze from love to love?"

"You know, my grandmother once said something. There are no hard, fast rules here. The norm is to love, then leave. That's the way it is."

"Always?"

"Yes."

"But you said it was the norm. Does that mean there were instances that didn't fit that norm?"

"There have been affairs where the parting was difficult for some."

"And? What did they do?"

"They each gave up their gift."

"What do you mean? How?"

"They simply stopped loving." A shadow crossed Sophie's face. "I'm sorry I brought it up, dear, none of those stories had happy endings."

"Well, you did bring it up. What kind of endings did they have?"

Sophie's fingers squeezed around Nikki's hand. "Not the kind I'd have you see."

"But Sophie—"

"Imagine a life without love."

The bleakness of her future stretched before Nikki like an endless black pit. "I don't know if it would be worth living."

Sophie turned over Nikki's hand and uncurled her fingers. "You must resolve yourself to the releasing. When you let go, it leaves you open to receive again."

"I—I don't know how to do that."

"It is the biggest sacrifice. When you can live your life for another's happiness, then you'll understand."

"And what of *my* happiness?"

"Of course you're entitled to that. We all are. Just remember, there's much happiness to be found in this world. Sometimes you have to hunt it down and sometimes you have to make it yourself. Often you'll find it where you least expect it."

Nikki's head pounded. She needed to find a quiet spot to go slowly insane. Even Sophie's sage advice wasn't helping. She pushed back from the table and stood. The desolation she'd first encountered with Dylan crushed down on her. "Well, right now I can't imagine ever feeling happy again."

She had almost reached the door when Sophie laid a hand on her shoulder, her eyes deep with concern. "Your young man has resisted the healing, but he has tasted the relief you bring. I have a feeling about this. You must prepare yourself."

"You think he'll be back?"

"Making love is just part of it with him. If you are to truly help him heal, you must get him to talk."

"How?"

The gray of Sophie's eyes brightened. "Why, that's easy. You listen."

WOULD DYLAN COME BACK TO HER?

The thought rolled through Nikki's mind for the hundredth time since her talk with Sophie. Nikki sipped her wine and banished the hope Sophie's words had instilled. She couldn't think about that. She'd go mad.

Instead she focused on the details of her kitchen: Tess's drying racks of herbs, Erin's candles and her own row of cat figurines sunning themselves on the windowsill. For all intents and purposes they'd created a home—temporary maybe, but a home nonetheless. She took a deep breath and smiled a small smile as her gaze drifted over her sisters—Erin sitting beside her and Tess sitting across the table beside Stefan, another former lover.

"It's a nice house. You should have come." Tess leaned toward Erin.

Nikki held her breath as Erin's shoulders rolled back in what had to be a bid for patience. "I had to meet with a client."

"And did that go well?" Nikki jumped in before Tess

could continue talking about the house. It was better to wait for Erin to show some interest on her own than to have her shoot down the idea because Tess badgered her.

"We signed a contract. It's a loft in Five Points. Lots of space, a decent budget."

"That's great." Nikki turned to Tess. "Isn't that great?"

"Wonderful. But she should have come with us the other day to see the house. Now *there's* a place that needs a little feng shui. Not that the fountain in the courtyard isn't a good start."

"You know enough of that to do it without me," Erin said.

Tess shook her head. "No one knows feng shui the way you do. This place is begging for your expert touch."

"Well, I'm moving away from all…that." Erin waved her hand.

"All what?" Both Nikki and Tess turned to her.

"All that…woo-woo stuff."

Tess frowned. "What woo-woo stuff?"

"New-agey, psychobabbly, out-there stuff."

"Like feng shui?" Nikki asked, amazed. Erin had always been the one to favor Sophie and her uncommon ways.

Erin nodded.

"Come on, Erin, you were the one who convinced Maggie to let you attend that feng shui workshop when you were just fourteen. You live for that stuff." Tess frowned at her.

"Not anymore." She glanced at Stefan, who sat silently chewing, then back at Tess. "And I'm certainly not buying into this sexual-healing malarkey."

Stefan stopped chewing to glance up, his eyes rounded with interest. "Sexual healing? Now you ladies are talking."

Tess gave his arm a squeeze. "Right, Stef, remember when you told me I had the magic touch?"

"Sure. I never thought of it before, but remember how I was allergic to just about everything before we met?"

"Right. You came into the nursery and you were all broken out in hives." She turned to her sisters. "He was so pitiful, I just couldn't resist him."

"Well, when was the last time I had an allergic reaction?"

Tess cocked her head. "I can't remember."

"Neither can I, but it's been close to a year, I'll bet. Not so much as a sniffle since we met." He nodded at Erin. "There you go. I'm living proof."

Erin's eyes narrowed on Stefan. "You don't actually think banging my sister cured your allergies?"

"First of all, I made love to your sister."

"Thank you, dear." Tess winked at him.

"*Banging* doesn't cut it. It was huge—even bigger than making love. I can't describe it." His gaze traveled over Tess. "And even though she's not my squeeze anymore, she's still very special to me. I've never had that with any other woman."

"Look, just because you two had a good love life does not mean the act had any effect on your health."

"Maybe, maybe not. Who's to say? I'm a new man and *I* think it's your sister's doing. There may be something to this sexual-healing thing."

"Great." With a scowl of dissatisfaction Erin stood. "That's just dandy. I'm so happy for all of you. I, for one, think you have a few loose screws."

"Erin, please stay. No need to get carried away here." Nikki patted her vacated chair.

"*I'm* getting carried away? The three of you are talking about healing men by having sex with them and I'm the unreasonable one?"

"Why is it so hard to believe?" Tess asked. "It explains everything. Puts Maggie's whole vagabond lifestyle into nice perspective."

"You know, I think not having any real roots has interfered with your common sense," Erin said.

"Come on, Erin, stick around. We'll change the subject," Nikki encouraged.

Erin shrugged. "I have stuff to do. I'll check you later."

After she left, Tess turned to Nikki. "We have got to do something about that girl. She spends way too much time alone."

"She's fine. Sophie thinks she just needs to grow into it. We'll talk to her about it later."

"Talking isn't her problem." Stef folded his arms across his chest.

"No?" Tess and Nikki asked in unison.

"No. I think it's very simple." He blessed them with his white smile. "Find her a man."

Nikki frowned. She'd found Dylan and what had that gotten her? Nightmares of standing helplessly by while he succumbed to Evelyn's schemes flooded her. Why had Nikki answered that door?

She turned to Tess. "I'm not so sure."

"No, he's right." Tess rubbed her hands together. "We'll pop our little sister right out of her funk. We'll find her a man."

"I THOUGHT YOU WERE E-MAILING that file." Dylan gritted his teeth the following Monday as he spoke to Evelyn in her office.

"I did e-mail it. It was a large file, though, so I thought you'd appreciate a hard copy." She shrugged. "She's quite lovely, in a homey kind of way."

"You had no business talking to her."

"Why? She answered your door. What was I supposed to do?"

"Just stay away from her. My personal affairs are none of your concern." He stormed toward his own office.

Damn it, he hadn't wanted Nikki to be tainted in any way by associating with his friends or family. Evelyn was poison. She'd befriended Kathy to a disastrous end. Nikki seemed too trusting to stand up to Evelyn's shenanigans.

He strode past Julie, waving aside her efforts to gain his attention, then slammed his door behind him. After he had dreamed of Kathy the other night, he'd run like a haunted schoolboy. He'd driven up the coast aimlessly, stopping at a hole-in-the-wall hotel somewhere past Boynton Beach. He'd worked all day, ignoring the burning sun and the distant roar of the ocean as he secluded himself in the musty room.

A lot of good it had done him. The hearing hadn't gone well. The councilman was now scheduled for trial.

Dylan shook his head. At least he'd managed not to call Nikki, though the urge to do so swamped him more frequently than ever. He had to get a grip. Even if she understood the limitations of their relationship, was it right for him to use her heavenly body to chase away his demons? And what good did it do if afterward he was haunted more than ever with feelings of betrayal?

"God, Kathy, I'm so sorry. It's just so damn hard without you."

A soft rap sounded at his door. He swallowed the bitterness in his throat. "Come in."

Julie entered and hovered tentatively in the doorway. "I'm sorry to disturb you, but your father needs to see you. He says it's urgent."

"Right." He straightened. Everything was urgent with the old man, but this had to be about the hearing. Weatherby pulled a lot of weight in this city, the kind of weight Mitchell Cain needed to keep up the lifestyle he was so accustomed to. "Please tell him I'll be right there."

She ducked her head and left. Dylan closed his eyes and summoned whatever store of patience he might have left. He could use a distraction right now, and his father, with his constant premonitions of disaster, might be what Dylan needed.

A few moments later he stood in the old man's office.

"The judge is fast-tracking this. It can't be a good thing." His father ran his hands through his graying hair and paced the length of the thick Persian rug covering the polished wood floor.

"I've got it under control. You don't need to worry."

"I'll damn well worry if I want to. Do you realize the importance of this case? Do you know exactly what George Weatherby is worth to us?"

Dylan stood stiffly beside the mahogany desk his father had had imported. "I'm sure you'll enlighten me."

"He's a paranoid son of a bitch who's got more money than he knows what to do with. The half a million plus in retainers and donations to key organizations we're involved with is nothing to him."

"According to his financial records, the bulk of it is in those donations."

"They're all aboveboard. Nothing the judge can get upset about." His father's eyes narrowed. "Just remember that we've done a lot of business with the councilman in the past. We need this trial tied up in a pretty bow as quickly as possible. If he goes down, it will reflect badly on this practice."

"So you think he's innocent?"

"What the hell kind of question is that?"

"You've known the man all these years. Is he guilty of fraud and/or extortion? Did he or did he not pressure those tenants into buying faulty appliances at triple the current retail price?"

"Of course he's innocent. He didn't do any such thing, and I expect you to discredit anyone who claims otherwise." Mitchell's expression dared Dylan to argue.

"Now, why would I doubt such a fine, upstanding citizen?"

"Look, you don't have to like the guy. You don't even have to believe in his innocence. You simply need to do your job. The prosecution doesn't have a case. The media is trying to make him out to be some slumlord. It's a farce. If he duped all those residents, then where's the money? His finances are clean as a whistle. You'll see. Justice will prevail. And when it does—" his gray gaze captured Dylan's "—well, I think there's room for another partner in this firm."

"I'll keep that in mind." Dylan stared at his father for a long moment. A few weeks ago he would have jumped at the opportunity, but somehow his father's bait had lost its appeal. Had meeting Nikki changed his priorities? He shook his head as he headed back to his office, his mind filled with thoughts of Nikki, her life…and sisters.

"WHAT ARE YOU TWO UP TO?" Erin eyed her sisters warily as they circled around her Monday evening. She sat in her favorite chair in the sunroom with her feet tucked under her and her book open in her lap.

Nikki really hoped Tess had found the right guy for Erin. She was the most wholesome looking of the three of them. With luck, this man was an intelligent guy who would appreciate her complex personality.

"We're not up to anything. What are you doing to-night?" Tess schooled her face into the picture of innocence she'd perfected at an early age.

"Yes, you are. You go around ignoring me for weeks, now all of a sudden I'm the center of attention."

"Oh, hon..." Nikki squeezed her shoulder. "I guess we've all been a little preoccupied lately. I never meant to ignore you."

"No big deal. It isn't like I need the two of you breathing down my neck. I've been plenty busy. I signed another client the other day."

"Well, of course you have. Good for you." Tess squatted beside the chair. "But since we haven't seen much of each other lately, we were hoping you'd hang with us tonight."

Erin's shoulders heaved in what seemed a bid for patience. She considered them silently, then finally set aside her book. "Okay, what did you have in mind?"

9

A FEW HOURS LATER, ERIN threw back her head and laughed, which prompted a sigh of relief from Nikki. Thank God Erin seemed to be enjoying herself. And she hadn't seemed to catch on when they'd *accidentally* run into Max, one of Tess's exes, and his friend. Of course, they were always running into Tess's exes.

For once, though, Erin had taken the encounter in stride. In fact, she and Ryan, the friend, seemed to be hitting it off.

"I can't believe how easy this has been." Tess leaned toward Nikki and spoke into her ear just loud enough for Nikki to hear over the hubbub of the bar and grill. "Why didn't we try this before?"

"I don't know, but when was the last time you saw her smile like that?"

Tess shrugged, then turned as Ramon stopped by the table. It always impressed Nikki how Tess's current lovers didn't seem to mind the never-ceasing presence of her minions. It seemed a little ironic that Dylan's lost love no longer walked this earth but Nikki burned with jealousy for the woman.

She gritted her teeth against a wave of longing. Dylan still hadn't called or made any attempt to see her. Had Sophie been wrong? It seemed he was truly gone from her life.

"Hey, Nikki, why so down?" Max touched her arm.

The look of concern on his face tightened her throat. She swallowed and forced a smile. "Nothing. I'm good."

"I heard you had a new man."

"*Had* being the operative word there."

He frowned slightly. "I'm sorry."

"Me, too."

"Hey, you two don't mind if we step out for a little fresh air? Ramon wants to show us his new car," Tess said.

Nikki shrugged. "Sure, go on. I'll hold down the fort." After they'd all left, she turned to Max. "Not interested in Ramon's car?"

"When I can have you all to myself?"

"Me and my sour mood."

"I can handle it."

"Tell me something. How did you do it?"

"Do what?"

"End things with my sister but...not."

A smile curved his lips. "Tess has a gift."

"So it seems. I don't see how she does it. I mean, how does she let go? How does she go from lover to friend like that?"

"I don't know. The time was right and it was all straight."

Just like Maggie. "I know. Still...was it real for you?"

"Our relationship?"

She nodded. Maybe it hurt so badly with Dylan because he was meant to be more than someone she healed.

"About the most real relationship I've ever had. I've never known anything like it." A smile curved his lips. "She opened me up somehow—helped me dig deeper. I've been with several women since Tess, none for very long, but each rocked me like when I was with your sister. Tess gave me that."

Nikki sat back in her chair, a feeling of defeat pressing down on her. Maybe she *was* defective. Her gift seemed to have manifested differently from her mother's or her sister's. It wasn't supposed to hurt like this.

"Hey, here they come." He nodded to the two couples—and indeed they were both couples at this point, with Erin's and Ryan's arms twined around each other—heading toward them.

"They look good together," Max said, indicating Erin and Ryan.

"Yes, thanks for helping to hook them up. She appears to be happy."

"What are you two saying about me?" Erin asked as Ryan held her chair for her.

"I'll never tell." Nikki straightened and pasted on another smile.

Did Erin have the gift? She'd had a few low-key relationships, but nothing that stuck in Nikki's mind. Was Erin able to move from lover to lover with the same ease Tess had mastered?

Everyone settled again at the table and Nikki did her best to relax and try to enjoy herself. Twice she jumped at the musical notes of a cell phone, but her own phone sat mutely in her bag.

Who was she kidding? Dylan wasn't going to call. The sooner she accepted that and got on with her life, the better.

"Hey." Erin leaned across the table. "I'm sorry I didn't come see your house."

"It's okay."

"No, really, I'd like to see it…if it's still okay."

"Sure. I'd like that. I'll call the agent tomorrow and make the arrangements."

Had she been relegated to the role of buyer in Dylan's life? Would her only contact with him now be regarding a land transaction?

She sipped her drink. Laughter and excited chatter floated around her. At least her sisters were enjoying the evening. She pretended to enjoy herself even as gloom pressed down around her.

Was Dylan truly healed? She glanced around the pub. Several men made eye contact and perked up immediately. It seemed she hadn't lost her touch. With just one look she could have any one of them by her side.

Was she a one-night wonder once more?

"Hey, you going to get that?" Tess asked.

Nikki started at the musical summons of her cell phone. She pawed through her bag, then held the phone to her ear. "Hello?"

"Nikki?"

"Yes?" Her heart thudded as she rose and moved toward the door, one finger pressed to her other ear as she tried to hear.

"It's Dylan. I know I ducked out on you the other morning and I'm sorry for that. I'll understand if you don't want anything to do with me now, but I…I need to see you."

THUNDER BOOMED. DARKNESS surrounded him and rain slashed his face. The squeal of tires reverberated in surreal tones through the night. He reached out, grasping thin air as his throat closed on his scream.

He stood helpless as the car skidded in slow motion, then slammed into the power pole, the boom of impact rising over the turbulence of the storm. His heart pounding, he ran toward the vehicle. Live cables fell from above, spraying sparks all around him. He froze as one of the lines dropped perilously close.

Then he was moving, pressing his hands to the glass of the driver's window, desperately peering inside. He yanked on the door handle, but the collision had bent the frame.

A bolt of lightning lit the sky, illuminating the figure in the car. The air bag had failed to deploy. Nikki lay lifeless and broken across the steering wheel.

His chest seized and he screamed.

"Dylan, wake up." Her soft voice floated over him.

Slowly he surfaced from the nightmare, the horror of

it clinging to him. He blinked her face into view. Nikki bent over him, vibrant and alive, her eyes filled with concern.

"It was just a dream," she soothed with her voice and her touch.

He turned his face into her palm and breathed in the clean scent of her while his heart galloped with dread.

"You want to talk about it?" She shifted beside him. He resisted the urge to sweep her into his arms, to lose himself once more in her magical charms.

"You dreamed about it...the accident?" she asked.

He pushed away from her, swinging his legs over the side of the bed. "What do you know about that?"

"That you once loved deeply and you lost her to a terrible accident."

"Who— It was Evelyn. She had no business telling you."

"She meant no harm."

He turned to face her, steeling himself against the sight of her. "Stay away from her."

"Look, I can handle Evelyn."

"I don't want you to handle her. I don't want you anywhere near her. We agreed to keep all personal stuff out of this."

"Why?" Her voice caught. "I know we made a deal, but I want to help. I can't do that if you don't talk to me."

The sweet tone of her words tempted him. His chest tightened as he met her gaze. The softness of her eyes melted some of his resolve. He inhaled, then blew out the breath in a rush. "She was amazing. You would have liked her."

Nikki didn't comment, just listened, her expression intent. She smoothed her hand along his arm and the warmth spread through him.

"I was in boarding schools since I was old enough for my parents to ship me off. I barely remember a time when I lived at home. Kathy and Steven were my family. As we grew older, well…Kathy was my home. She was all I ever needed."

He was silent for a long moment, drifting through the memories: the first time he saw her, with her pigtails and clenched fists; the night they first declared their love; how she squirmed and laughed when he kissed the hollow of her back, then begged him to do it again.

"She was like a kid with her love of life, her exuberance. Steven, my first boarding school roommate, he hated that he'd met her first but she ended up with me." He shook his head. "Now he's the married one, the happy one."

He fell again into silence, a small sense of wonder filling him. He could talk about her and it didn't hurt. He let his gaze travel over Nikki. "I'm sorry, that's probably the last thing you want to hear about."

Tears shimmered in her eyes and he froze. What an oaf. He'd upset her.

But she smiled and touched him then, and he became lost again in the magic of her.

NIKKI HUMMED SOFTLY AS SHE scrubbed for surgery the next morning. She'd listened, the way Sophie advised, and Dylan had opened up to her. Sophie had been right about so many things.

Could she be right about Nikki finding happiness?

Dylan had come back to her. And this time it felt more like a beginning than an end. He'd been more tender than ever, waking her early and making sweet love to her before they started the day.

He'd made her promise to return tonight. How could she refuse? She'd been there for him last night and he'd talked about Kathy.

Maybe now he'd start to let her go.

"WHAT ARE YOU DOING?" Nikki asked as she nearly stumbled over Tess, who stood in the hall with her ear pressed to Erin's bedroom door that Saturday night.

"Shush." Tess waved her on and continued her intent eavesdropping.

"No way." Nikki grabbed her by the arm and pulled her down the hall. "That is so rude." A loud thump sounded from Erin's room. Nikki glanced back in spite of herself. "What's going on in there?"

"Lots of moaning and groaning and these cooing—"

"Don't tell me. I don't want to know. It is none of our business."

"Sure it is. If not for us, she wouldn't be in there with that hottie, Ryan."

"That does not give you the right to listen at her door."

"But they've been in there since Tuesday night. That's four days. I don't think either of them has stepped a foot out of that room the entire time. I'm pretty sure he hasn't."

"Since Tuesday?"

"Yeah. If they keep this up much longer, they may come close to breaking my personal record."

"Really?" Nikki's surprise increased. "And exactly what is that record? No, never mind. I don't think I really want to know."

"Remember that cruise I took with Lewis Baker last year? The one where we sailed to— Hell, I don't remember where we sailed. I hardly saw the outside of the cabin once we left the port."

Nikki frowned. Which one of the many men who had passed through her sister's life in the past year had been Lewis? It wasn't as if Nikki kept a scorecard. "You mean the redhead with the great buns?"

Tess rolled her eyes. "People kept asking if we were brother and sister. What a bunch of sickos. We were practically joined at the hip, if not lip-locked whenever we were in public. He used to say he wanted the world to know I was his. He loved public displays and really liked having sex in risky places. While we were on that cruise—"

"Too much information." Nikki shook her head. "I think I remember him. Was that over the Fourth of July weekend?"

"We left on Wednesday and got back Monday." Tess wiggled her eyebrows suggestively.

"You...the entire time?" Nikki asked, amazed in spite of herself.

"Five and a half days."

Before Nikki could reply, Erin's door scraped open and their youngest sister stumbled into the hall. She shut the door quickly behind her, then straightened and smoothed down her hair when she spotted them. The attempt did little to tame the wild mass of blond curls framing her flushed face. "What are you two up to?"

Tess swaggered back like an offended sailor, puffing her chest out and fisting her hands on her hips. "Why do you always think we're up to something?"

"Because you always are."

Nikki stepped between them before sparks began to fly. She glanced at the closed door. "So everything going okay?"

Erin's eyes flashed. "Of course everything's fine. Why wouldn't everything be fine?"

"No reason." Nikki frowned. "Just asking."

"Well, everything is absolutely dandy. I'm just going to get...to get us something to drink."

"So that *is* Ryan you're hoarding away in there?" Tess tried to peer past her.

"Of course it's Ryan. Who else would I have back there? Unlike some people, I'm a one-man-at-a-time kind of girl—"

"And what does that mean?" Tess glared threateningly at her younger sister.

Nikki gripped Tess's arm. "Look, why don't we all get some nice cool lemonade?"

Farther up the hall, Tess's door scraped open and Ramon leaned out. "You girls having a party?"

"Hey, who drank all the lemonade?" Max stood at the end of the hall holding an empty pitcher.

Stefan moved in beside Max. "Did someone say something about a party?"

Erin gestured toward the men. "Does anyone else see something wrong with this picture?"

"What exactly is your problem, Erin? Just when I think you're loosening up and learning to enjoy yourself—"

"Tess. Erin. Let's not do this. It's late. We should all get some sleep," Nikki said. When had life here turned into such a circus?

Erin stepped up to Max and snatched the pitcher from him. "I'll take this, thank you."

"Hey, want me to fill that up with something else for you? I think there was some orange juice." He gestured toward the kitchen, but Erin had already turned away. Without saying another word, she disappeared into her room, shutting the door behind her.

"She attacked me. Did you see that?" Tess asked. "I'm not imagining it."

"Come to bed, my sweet." Ramon reached for her and, thankfully, she went to him. "Let me hold you. I want to tell you about the time I fell in love with this beautiful redhead."

He pulled Tess into the room with him, murmuring softly to her as the door closed behind them.

For a moment Nikki stood in the darkened hall. Max and Stef had gone into the living room, where, from the sound of it, they were watching late-night reruns of a reality show. She leaned against the wall as the moaning began again in Erin's room and muffled laughter sounded through Tess's bedroom wall.

Even as a pang of envy gripped her, Nikki couldn't help wondering. Things just weren't like the old days anymore. It seemed that the more men they had in their lives, the further apart the three of them grew. Though Erin had asked to see the house, they hadn't been able to work out a time between their schedules. Sadness settled over Nikki.

Had the three of them outgrown each other?

10

"It's natural that the three of you should each find your own way." Thomas blew out a puff of smoke from the pipe he'd favored for years.

Nikki always knew when he was taking a break by the smell of tobacco that circled his work area. Thomas was as fond of sitting down for a long smoke and contemplating the intricacies of life as he was of tinkering in his workshop. She'd woken up in a funk that Sunday. Unable to shake it all day, she'd gone for a late-afternoon drive, ending up at his house.

"I guess you're right. I never thought about it before. It's kind of sad."

"You'll each get caught up in your own lives. Knowing you girls, you'll still be close, but just like you'll learn to let go of the men in your life, you'll learn to let go of your sisters in a way."

She nodded. Was Thomas right? Erin was already spending so much time away from them. And Tess… well, it was always hard to tell what Tess might do. She was so much like their mother. "I guess. Maggie never stayed in one place for more than a few months. She painted and she loved. It seemed she threw herself into a new painting each time she took a new lover. Then one day she'd announce that she was done with her latest masterpiece. That usually coincided with the end of the affair. Though I never liked it, I did get used to it."

"Do you ever miss her?"

She glanced up at him and frowned. "Who? Maggie?"

"Yes, your mother. Do you miss her?"

Nikki sat back and frowned some more. Did she miss Maggie? "I never thought about it."

"Missing someone isn't something you have to think about. It just happens. Either you do or you don't."

She stared for a moment at the small fan behind him that made a feeble attempt to stir the heavy air. "You know we never got along so well. All my memories of her are of us fighting or of her being disappointed in me—or me in her. I think it's more like relief when she isn't around."

His gaze fixed on her, keen and probing. "Even now that you're grown?"

She shrugged. "Well…I think with recent revelations I understand her a little better, so maybe that means we'd get along. She isn't around much to tell."

"But she will be. She always comes back. Do you think the two of you might stand a chance then?"

Years of resentment rose in her, swirling in a confusion with her honest desire to get to know the woman who had raised her. "She's never been much of a mother figure—thank God for you and Sophie—but maybe it would be nice to have a peaceful relationship with her."

"The problem is you're every bit as hardheaded as she is." He paused to savor his pipe, then said, "She'd like to start fresh with you—with all of you girls."

"Really? You've spoken with her…while she's been abroad?"

"A few times. We e-mail pretty regularly."

"And she talks about us?"

"She talks about a lot of things, but, yes, she talks about you girls. I told her about the house you're buying."

"She must have laughed at that. She never understood why I wanted to settle in one place. 'Expand your horizons,' she'd say."

"She was very proud of you, actually." He stopped to pack more tobacco into the pipe from a small leather pouch at his side. "I don't think she ever stopped to think about how her lifestyle didn't suit you. I think she's sorry for that."

Nikki sat silent for a moment, nursing all the old hurts. "I guess she couldn't change who she was."

She stood and paced out the open garage door to the fence, where a half-beaten rug lay cooking in the heat. "Maybe if I didn't expect her to be a mother, maybe if I thought of her more as a friend…"

Thomas shook his head. "But she is your mother whether you can accept that or not. It would be nice if you could. You know, there's no set definition of what a mother should be. She birthed you. She did her best to care for you when you were growing up. Maybe she isn't the best by your standards, but you could have done a lot worse."

Nikki nodded. "I know, Thomas." She paced back into the shaded interior. "I always had such different expectations. Other kids had normal, stable homes. Why couldn't we?"

"You know what Sophie would say?"

A small smile crept across her lips. "Something about how there is no such thing as a normal family and how we each plan our lives before we come here and we pick the families who best serve whatever lessons we have for this lifetime."

He sat back and grinned. "Yep, that's exactly what she'd say."

"So what lesson am I supposed to be learning?"

He shrugged. "You'll have to go to Sophie for that. I'm still trying to figure it all out."

"So any idea when we'll see Maggie?"

"You know how she is. We'll see her when the time is right. Seems to me we're getting close, though."

"Time for her to cut this one loose?"

"They're all different, but I've got that feeling. She's starting to let go."

"Really?" Nikki sat forward. "How can you tell?"

"By the tone of her voice, the things she says…"

"What do you mean her tone of voice?"

"When she's in that first flush of love, her tone is very light—you know, ecstatic. She's in that infatuation phase. Then as the relationship progresses, she kind of blooms, then mellows. I've talked her through years of relationships. I think I've gotten a feel for it."

"So what kinds of things does she say when the relationship gets near the end?"

"She makes fewer references to time in connection with that person. No mention of future plans. Then there's the most obvious clue."

"What's that?"

"The pronoun shift."

Nikki peered at him expectantly.

"Singular as opposed to plural. Instead of *we're* enjoying France, it's *I'm* enjoying France."

"I see. It's a verbal distancing of sorts."

"I don't even think she's aware of it."

"You know her so well." How long had Thomas been in the wings for Maggie? "I still don't see why the two of you never hooked up. Are you impervious to her charms?"

He looked at her a long moment as a smile curved his lips. "Guess the time was never right."

"Thomas—" Nikki regarded him "—are you telling me you think there might be a right time for you and Maggie?"

"This McClellan gift is something to deal with."

"You're not telling *me* anything new."

"You having a hard time with it?"

A short, derisive laugh burst from her. "Seems I'm still handicapped in the letting go department."

He nodded, his look intense. "I've been thinking

about that. Seems to me the letting go might have something to do with the way you love."

"How so?"

"Think about Maggie and Tess—even Sophie for that matter, though you probably don't see that part of her—they love with abandon, with their hearts and arms wide open."

"So you're saying that I'm close-hearted, that I'm clingy?"

"No, sweetie, but you are so intense sometimes. You love with a fierce protectiveness. It's beautiful and full, but it may be more harmful in the long run."

"But…how do I love with abandon? I don't get that. What does that even mean? I don't see how they can truly love someone so completely, then move on at the drop of a hat."

"But that they do, all right."

"Well, I don't know how, Thomas. I'm beginning to think I got miswired somewhere along the way."

"Tell me, with this young man of yours…you've been holding back?"

"What do you mean?"

"Have you let yourself fall in love with him?"

Had she fallen in love with Dylan? "I don't know. I get this rush anytime he calls or when I see him. And I miss him loads when I don't see him. But I keep thinking each time could be the last. I don't understand why he's been different than the others, why he's still around." She laughed. "*If* he's still around. I don't even know. I take it one day at a time. If we make plans, I take them with a grain of salt and half expect him to cancel or no-show."

She closed her eyes and fisted her hands in her hair. "I don't believe I've ever made it to that plural-pronoun stage in a relationship. Maybe I never will. Maybe it'll just always be *me* and *him* and never *us*. You know this history I have—the one-shot wonder. God, I sound so insecure."

"Sweetie, you don't sound insecure. You sound like you're trying your best to hang loose and see what might happen next."

"Yeah. That's exactly what I'm trying to do."

"But you're hesitant. Understandably so. You're afraid to put too much of yourself into something that might not last."

"Sure. I'll admit to that, but it doesn't help that he doesn't seem eager to put anything of himself out there either. I thought we were making progress. He was starting to open up, but now I don't know. He seems more closed than ever. It's like one step forward, two steps back." She plopped down next to Thomas on the old car seat he kept in his workroom. "So what do I do to keep my sanity through all this? Because sometimes I feel like I'm falling off the deep end."

"Well, sweetie…" He freed a strand of sweat-dampened hair from the side of her face and tucked it behind her ear. "Maybe you should just loosen up and not worry about falling in love. I mean, it's kind of like missing someone—either you love a person or you don't. It's a given. I don't think any of us has an option there. Maggie and Tess can't help that they love heart and soul each time."

She squinted as the sun's rays sank even with the fence outside the door, blurring the lines of the rug. "Thomas, do you think Dylan may still be in my life because I haven't allowed myself to fall in love with him, so he hasn't benefited fully from any healing power I might have?"

"He's still around because he isn't healed yet?"

She turned to him. "Yes…because I'm afraid to love him."

His eyebrows arched and he took a long pull on the pipe, then cocked his head back and let the smoke curl in a lazy puff from his mouth. "Could be."

"So if I really want to help him, I have to get over being afraid of losing him and I have to let myself fall in love with him?"

"I don't have the answers, Nikki. Like I said, I don't think any of us has a choice in who we love." His eyes took on a far-off look, and for the very first time she wondered if Thomas had ever loved anyone. Then he straightened and turned to her. "I would caution you, though, before you go tumbling head over heels. Make sure you're good and ready. I have a feeling when you fall in love, you'll fall hard."

She turned back to where the sun painted the horizon

brilliant red, orange and gold. Thomas was probably right. The question was, had she already started that fall?

COLD CURLED AROUND NIKKI and she shivered as she surfaced into consciousness. The early-morning light fell through an opening in the curtain, pooling on the soft carpet. A dog barked somewhere in the distance and a lawn mower rumbled to life.

For the briefest moment she braced herself for the feeling of abandonment, but then she relaxed, glancing over at the empty space beside her. Dylan had left his bed but not the house. She could sense his presence. A bump from somewhere downstairs confirmed that he was having trouble sleeping again.

She rubbed her arms and slipped from the bed, wrapping the sheet around her. She followed the sounds to the formal living room. Light from a side table softly illuminated him as he bent over a pile of ornate frames, candlesticks and other knickknacks. His mood was as jumbled as ever. The sadness still churned below the surface, but he seemed otherwise preoccupied. He'd slipped on a pair of shorts, and for just a moment she stood and looked her fill at the strong lines of his back and shoulders.

Would she ever tire of the sight of him?

"Hi," she said.

He straightened, his eyes wide in surprise. "Nikki, I'm sorry. Did I wake you?"

"What are you doing?"

"Well…" He rubbed his neck as if he wasn't quite sure himself. "I was just thinking that we've got the inspection coming up next week and the closing not far after that. I should start making plans…about where I'm going, what to do with all this."

"Oh." She hadn't thought about the closing. And she'd tried very hard not to think about him leaving this house. "There isn't any hurry. I haven't even begun to think about the move."

He blew out a breath, and for a moment they were silent. He shook his head. "I may just put everything into storage and rent some place until I figure out where I'm going. I'll call some movers today, see what I can schedule."

She nodded, though all she wanted to do was beg him to stay. "I have my apartment for a few more months still. I'll probably break the lease, depending on what my sisters do. So like I said, no hurry."

"You should start bringing your things over." He shrugged. "You're staying here half the time. You might as well have some clothes at least. There's plenty of room in the closet, and I could clear out part of the dresser."

"I suppose that makes sense." She kept her voice calm, though excitement raced through her. What would it be like to live with him—share this house with him?

He stepped over to her and took her into his arms. "You'll stay again tonight? We'll spend the day together. Just the two of us. Maybe head to the beach for a long swim, then come back here and make love until we're exhausted. We can stop by your place and pick up a load of your things while we're out."

"I'd like that."

"Ah, Nikki…" He tilted her head and kissed her, his lips firm and warm. She opened to him and his tongue stroked hers with gentleness.

His hands skimmed her, and the sheet pooled at her feet. He broke the kiss and moved back to let his gaze sweep over her. "You know I want you all the time. When I'm with you, it seems I can hardly get enough of you. And when we're apart, all I can think about is being with you again. Of being inside you again."

She pulled him to her, pressing her body against the muscular wall of his torso. He caressed her back as he kissed her again, taking her mouth with more urgency. She wrapped her arms around him and held on as he pulled her slowly to the floor.

"Let me love you, Nikki. Let me give to you," he murmured as he cupped her breast. His breath was warm, his mouth hot as he kissed her there, kneading her as he worked his tongue over her nipple, teasing it into an aching point.

She clasped her hands in his hair and gave herself up to the currents of desire flowing through her. Her blood warmed. Her sex pulsed. He moved from one breast to the other, suckling her for an endless time, until she moaned with need.

At last he nudged her knees apart and dipped his fingers between the swollen folds of her femininity. She sighed his name, and he took her mouth again as he thrust deep inside her. Her hips undulated of their own accord and she lost herself to the sensation as he drifted down her body, touching, tasting and teasing her with his lips and tongue. Finally he settled his mouth over her nether lips and kissed her deeply, thoroughly, exploring every inch of her swollen flesh before centering on her clit. His tongue drew circles of indescribable pleasure around her, sending prickles of heat dancing along her skin.

She ground against him, her movements growing more frenzied as the tension coiled through her and the heat built to an almost intolerable level. He thrust his fingers inside her while he laved her clit, his rhythm steady, even as the first tendrils of orgasm rippled outward through her.

"Ahh…Dylan." She closed her eyes as a rainbow of light burst along her body. She cried out, her muscles stiffening as her climax took her.

He moved up and held her, stroking her back, until her breathing leveled out. She lay limp and sated, smiling lazily up at him.

He laughed. "You look like the cat that got the cream."

"Yes, sir. Now please take me back to bed and make proper love to me, so we can both bask in this lovely afterglow."

11

HE WASTED NO TIME IN complying, and when he slipped inside her moments later, it was all she could do not to cry out with the joy of it. He loved her well into the morning, taking his sweet time, thrusting with deep, sure strokes, until he shuddered and tensed and the climax carried them both to a place full of peace and light.

For long moments afterward, he lay covering her, his weight welcome. She smiled and lightly drew her nails up his back. "Yes, I think I would like very much to move some of my things in."

He rolled off her but scooped one arm around her and held her close against him. "I'd like that, too."

"I could help you pack, if you'd like."

His gaze grew serious. "There's something you should know about this house… It's very special. I'm telling you this because I know you'll care for it and appreciate it the way I do."

"I will. It's a wonderful house—full of light and space. It's the most beautiful one I've ever seen. I still don't know how you can bring yourself to part with it."

"Like I said before, it's time to move on. This house

was a chapter in my life that has come to a close. I can't hold on to it any longer."

She took his hand. "Because you shared it with Kathy?"

"That's part of it, but there's more...." His gaze swept the room from the arched entry to the crown molding. "There's a part of me in these walls." He focused on her. "I didn't always aspire to be an attorney. In fact, I would have done anything not to follow in my old man's footsteps."

The sadness loomed in him again, but she stroked his hand until it abated as he said, "Steven and I used to study architecture together. My parents pitched a fit when they found out, threatened to transfer me to another school."

He shook his head at the memory. "I couldn't bear the thought of being separated from Kathy and Steven, so I bucked up and went into prelaw like a good son."

"I'm so sorry, Dylan."

"It's okay. I actually enjoyed it in those days, before I started practicing. You know, it's all so idealistic on paper. Defending the innocent and all that. In real life...well, it's not as satisfying as I'd have hoped."

"It doesn't have to be that way."

"It's where I am now, and for once in my life I'm doing something my family is proud of."

"But you don't seem overly happy about that."

"My family carries a lot of influence in their little arena of the world. As long as I stay on their good side, I have the potential of achieving great success in life."

"But you should be happy in what you do, Dylan. If practicing law doesn't fulfill you, then why not try something else?"

"This house—" he made a broad sweeping gesture "—it was my one big foray outside of law."

She followed his gaze around the room. "You mean you designed this? You're the architect?"

"With Steven's help, of course. I could never have carried it off without him."

"But the design is yours."

"I knew what I wanted. It wasn't that hard to get it down on paper. The execution was murder. I had already started at my father's firm, so I worked around a pretty grueling schedule. It took almost a year and a half of my life seeing it to fruition. I can't tell you how many times I almost gave up."

"And your parents didn't approve?"

"I had a big housewarming when it was finished. I wanted them to come see it just once."

"What happened?"

"Not only did they not show but also half the guest list didn't. Seems no one was going to encourage my wayward behavior without their approval."

"That's so wrong."

"That's my world, Nikki. It's all a big political game. They were sending me a clear message that if I pursued a career outside of law, they'd never support it. They'd take all their backing and contacts. I never would have made it."

"So you decided to play by their rules."

"I had asked Kathy to marry me. I wanted to give her the life she deserved."

"But surely she would have supported your efforts to go out on your own?"

"It wasn't good enough for me. She deserved better. I would have had to go back to school, spend time in an apprenticeship. It was too late to start over."

"That's so sad, Dylan."

His shoulders heaved and the gloom pressed around him like a fog. "It is what it is. I just thought you might like to know."

"But what about now? Who's to say you couldn't start over now?" She gestured to the four walls. "This house is amazing. If this is what you can do as an amateur, what might you be capable of with the full training?"

"I don't know. None of it seems to matter anymore."

"It does matter." She cupped his face. "*You* matter, Dylan. Do you know why I'm here in your life?"

"To brighten it?"

"Exactly. I'm here to help you find happiness. That's my solemn belief."

"But you do make me happy, Nikki." The sincerity in his eyes sent warmth curling through her.

"Then promise me something."

"What?"

"Promise me you'll think about making a new start. Maybe taking some classes on architecture, at least part-time to see if you still like it."

"I'll think about it."

"Good. Meanwhile, let's not worry too much over this whole move thing. Especially now that I know about this house, it just doesn't seem right to have you move out. At least not until you're good and ready, which I hope won't be for a long while."

He frowned. "I was thinking…either way, I'd like to clear out most of the stuff in this place. You were right when you first came here and you said I didn't seem the claw-foot type."

She propped her head up on his shoulder and waited for him to continue. Her heart thudded. Was he ready to start clearing out some of Kathy's belongings?

"Kathy decorated this house. I gave her free rein and it made her happy, but I've never really felt at home here. It always seemed more her place than ours. Except for my study, the house has her brand on it. I think I'll give it all away—have a yard sale or something. Start fresh when I get to my new place."

"A yard sale?"

"Sure, why not? Want to help?"

Joy swelled up inside her. She grinned. "I thought you'd never ask."

DYLAN PUSHED ASIDE THOUGHTS of Nikki the following Wednesday morning. Her excitement about the yard sale had been infectious, and for the past few days he'd been caught up in the preparations. But he couldn't think about that now. He had to focus on the judge.

"Due to the current insufficiency of evidence, this case is dismissed." Judge Albright cast a stern glance at Dylan as the courtroom erupted in excited chatter.

Dylan nodded stiffly to the judge. The man didn't seem any happier about this outcome than Dylan was. Sure, it was great to win the case, but he couldn't feel good about this one. He'd found a bartender who testified the prosecution's key witness had been plastered on the night in question.

Dylan had hated discrediting the man, especially when he had a feeling that all was not well in the councilman's world. Yet, as his father had pointed out, there had been no money—no hidden accounts—and Dylan had had the best investigators looking for it.

Turning to Weatherby, Dylan offered his hand in congratulations. Weatherby pumped his hand with enthusiasm. "I knew you could do it, son. Never doubted you."

If only Dylan could shake his doubt of the councilman. "I did the job as I saw fit."

"Well, this will be a real feather in your cap. Your daddy's bound to be real proud."

"No doubt. Congratulations, Councilman. I'm sure you'll enjoy your victory. If you'll excuse me." He left the crowded courtroom as quickly as possible.

"Mr. Cain…" A dark-haired man approached him as he hit the courthouse steps. "Mike Peterson, *Miami Herald.* Great job you did in there. Do you have a comment for the paper, sir?"

Dylan stopped and faced the reporter. How could he

respond when he knew in his gut that Weatherby was guilty? He drew a deep breath. "No comment."

"No comment? But this is a tremendous victory."

Dylan paused, then turned back to the man, a neat smile on his face. At least this he could be truthful about. "Yes, I'm sure my father will be very proud."

He walked away. At least now that the case was over he could plan his upcoming move. If anything, he'd lose himself in packing. Beyond that, his future seemed fuzzy. He squared his shoulders and allowed himself to again focus on Nikki and the yard sale. Yes, it was high time he cleaned house.

THE MORNING OF THE YARD sale dawned bright and humid. Nikki woke before Dylan. She tied her hair back in a ponytail, then hurried to put out the signs they'd painted on neon poster board.

The aroma of fresh-brewed coffee hit her when she returned and stepped inside the coolness of the kitchen. Dylan kissed her soundly, and she closed her eyes to focus on the jumble of emotions flowing from him. There, buried below the excitement of the kiss, was a bittersweet sadness at the parting of old ways. Yet he was ready. His resolve to move forward was there, too.

They were doing the right thing.

He pulled back and the surety of it shone in his eyes. They had barely sipped from their coffee when the doorbell rang and the early-morning yard-salers hit them in force.

"Let me show you some paintings you might like." Dylan escorted a smiling couple through the open entryway hours later as Nikki poured lemonade for a mother and her young daughter.

"It looks empty in here." The girl spun around the spacious dining room.

"Most of the furniture sold within the first couple of hours." Nikki glanced around the vacant space.

Dylan had said he was ready to clean house and it seemed he'd meant it. She cocked her head toward the low rumble of his voice drifting in from the other room. So far he seemed at peace, maybe even excited about the evacuation of so much that Kathy had held dear.

He walked past carrying one end of the heavily framed painting of the Victorian lady in her garden. Nikki caught his eye and he winked. "I'll be right back. I'm going to help them run this over to their place. They're just a few streets over."

"I'll be here."

He glanced at the empty dining room and smiled. Yes, the thrill of a fresh start ran strong and clear through him.

"Do you have any vases?" The mother looked hopefully around.

"There's an assortment of knickknacks on the tables in the garden." Nikki walked them through the French doors to where they'd set up tables and shelves to display the assortment of odds and ends Kathy had collected.

"So you've made great progress, I see." Evelyn

Rogers appeared in the French doors, looking cool and pristine in a bright summer dress.

Nikki brushed a dust bunny from the hem of her cut-offs and dredged up a smile. A chill ran through her. What was Evelyn up to? "Evelyn, how nice of you to drop by Dylan's yard sale."

Evelyn smiled graciously and gestured to the array of household goods. "This is your doing?"

"He was ready. I just encouraged him. He wants to clean out the entire house, so it's out with the old, in with the new." She shrugged. "At least, out with the old for now. He's still deciding on a new place."

"Right. Nick and I were shocked when we saw the For Sale sign. I didn't think Dylan would ever part with this house."

"Nick?"

"My fiancé. There he is." She pointed past the French doors to the front door beyond, where a dark-haired man browsed over the assorted tables they'd placed along the front walkway.

"He's very handsome."

"Thanks. We've both been impressed by your effect on Dylan. I can't believe you've gotten him to clean house like this."

"I'm not sure what his plans are, but I'm sure he'll end up wherever he's meant to be. As for now, I think it's a good sign that he's ready to do away with most of this."

"That's wonderful, Nikki. It has to be a good sign that

he's ready to move on. Good for you, no doubt." Though the woman kept a sincere tone, malice oozed from her.

Nikki straightened. Whatever Evelyn was up to, it wasn't in Dylan's best interest. "It's good for *him*. Wherever he ends up, he's ready to move forward in a positive direction."

"Well, he should have plenty of time to make plans now that his big case is a wrap."

"Yes, I heard about that." Nikki stifled her disappointment. She'd seen an article in the *Miami Herald* about Councilman Weatherby's acquittal. She'd congratulated Dylan, but he'd barely acknowledged the comment.

"It's so exciting. He's worked forever for this. It's about time he made partner."

"Partner?"

"He hasn't mentioned it?"

"We don't— He doesn't say much about his work." Nikki had to be patient. It seemed one day he was ready to open up but the next he was silent again.

"Oh." Evelyn frowned. "Dylan has always been a little odd. Anyway, what are you wearing?"

Nikki glanced down at her T-shirt and shorts. "Just grunge clothes. It's been pretty dusty—"

"No, silly, to the gala."

"Gala?"

"Well, I suppose if he didn't say much about the case, it's no surprise he hasn't mentioned this."

"No, I guess not."

"So like a man." Evelyn shook her head. "His parents are throwing a huge bash next Saturday night. You have to come."

The coldness around her intensified. Goose bumps prickled up Nikki's arms. "I don't know. If he wanted me to come, he would have said so."

"I'm sure it's just an oversight. Besides—" she moved up beside Nikki "—*I'm* inviting you." Ill will spiked outward from the woman.

Nikki stiffened. "Can you do that?"

"I'm practically part of the family. I've helped Lillian, Dylan's mother, plan the thing from the start. Don't you worry about Dylan. I'll handle him. He's been hiding you away from everyone for long enough. Don't you think his parents will want to meet the woman responsible for his return to the land of the living?"

"I don't know." Dylan would be furious with her for going. Was that Evelyn's intent—to lure Nikki there so Dylan would be upset enough to break things off with her for good? Nikki stifled a rueful laugh. If Evelyn understood the transient nature of Nikki and Dylan's relationship, she wouldn't feel the need to trouble herself.

But what if Evelyn planned something else—something that would interfere with Dylan's healing?

"I insist. Lillian would never forgive me otherwise. She's dying to meet you."

"She is?"

"Oh yes. I've told her all about you."

Nikki glanced around at the tables of Kathy's goods.

She and Dylan had been making halting progress in their relationship, but it wasn't enough to facilitate the healing process. Maybe meeting his family would give her the edge she needed to help him overcome his past.

"So what do you say? You going to help me look good to Lillian and Mitchell by letting me be the one to introduce them to their son's mystery woman?"

What would become of her relationship with Dylan if Nikki unlocked the mystery of his past and he was truly healed? She closed her eyes against the crushing inevitability that her time with him was nearing its end. Would she be ready to let him go? She had a duty to see this through. Besides, whatever Evelyn planned, it didn't bode well for Dylan. If Nikki stuck close enough to the woman, maybe she could prevent the trouble Evelyn planned.

She drew a deep breath and faced Evelyn. "Okay, I'll go."

_12_

NIKKI SQUEEZED HER KNEES together to keep them from knocking. The glow of sequins and diamonds seemed to spread in every direction, muted only by the ever-present black tuxedos and evening dresses. She glanced down at her emerald dress, glad for once not to be wearing the requisite black. Raising her head high, she moved into the crowd gathered beyond the entry.

She'd come to look after Dylan, meet his family and friends and find out what Evelyn was plotting. There was no backing out now.

Someone touched her elbow and she turned to find Evelyn, resplendent in a ruby-colored gown, her platinum locks neatly coiled and pinned.

"Nikki, I'm ecstatic you came. I thought that you might not."

"I nearly didn't." In the end her fear for Dylan had propelled her out the door.

Evelyn nodded toward Nikki's dress. "You look smashing. You're sure to get a reaction out of our guy in that."

Our guy. A shiver of foreboding swept over Nikki.

Somehow Evelyn's friendly comment didn't quite seem so friendly.

Evelyn *did* want Dylan for herself. But at what price to him?

"Where's that gorgeous fiancé of yours?" Nikki asked, keeping her tone light.

Evelyn's smile faltered. "He's around."

"So how are the wedding plans coming?"

"Too many pesky details. I have a marvelous wedding coordinator who has it all in hand, though. Come on, let me introduce you around." She hooked her arm through Nikki's and led her toward a knot of people standing near open French doors. "Here, we might as well dive right in. That is Dylan's mother."

"Evelyn, aren't you going to introduce me?" A red-haired man with green eyes intercepted them before they reached the cluster by the doors.

"Steven, aren't you looking sharp tonight?"

"Oh, is this *the* Steven?" Nikki turned to him with a smile.

"That depends. Which Steven are you looking for?" He returned her smile as warmth emanated from him. She liked him immediately.

"Nikki, this is Steven Benson. He and Dylan go way back."

"Best friends for as far back as I can remember." He took her hand and his eyes widened. "Nikki? You're not *the* Nikki?"

She laughed. "That depends—"

"Yes, this is Dylan's Nikki."

Steven pumped her hand with much enthusiasm. "Oh my God, this is a thrill. Come here." He swept her into a bear hug. "I can't believe Rebecca missed you."

"Rebecca?" Nikki laughed again as he let her go but squeezed her hands.

"My wife. We've both been dying to meet you, but Dylan has been way too stingy with you. I'm so glad he brought you tonight."

"Well…I didn't actually come with Dylan—"

"She's *my* guest tonight." Evelyn took her by the arm. "I promised Lillian a surprise and I intend to provide one."

"You'd better watch your back with this one, Nikki." Steven's eyebrows drew together. He kept his tone light, though she sensed the true warning behind his teasing. "With all of them, actually."

"Don't be absurd. I'll take good care of her."

"That's what I'm afraid of."

"If you'll excuse us." Evelyn turned Nikki toward Lillian and her group. "Don't listen to him. He's just trying to make you nervous."

"Wait." Steven placed a business card in Nikki's hand. "If you ever need me for anything, you let me know. Any woman who can tolerate that ornery friend of mine is worth her weight in gold."

"Thank you, Steven."

"You have to promise to come and visit sometime. Becca is going to hate that she missed you, but she just couldn't make it tonight."

"I promise." She tucked the card in her bag as Evelyn directed her toward Dylan's mother.

"Lillian," Evelyn said to the sedate blonde as they neared. "You must meet Nikki McClellan."

Something in the shape of the woman's eyes reminded Nikki of Dylan, though Lillian's gaze held none of the warmth of her son's. A chill ran up Nikki's spine. It was difficult to picture this woman in a nurturing role. Nothing maternal emanated from her.

"Is it *Nicole* then?" she asked.

Nikki offered her hand. "Actually it's Nikki."

"I see." The woman offered a two-fingered shake, as though she disdained further contact.

Evelyn leaned in closer, as though she were indulging a secret. "This is *Dylan's* Nikki."

"Oh." Lillian peered at her with new interest.

"Nikki, this is Dylan's mother, Lillian Cain."

"Mrs. Cain, it's a pleasure to meet you."

"Come now, we'll have none of that. It's Lillian, dear. No need to make me feel any older than necessary. Mrs. Cain was my mother-in-law, God rest her soul. So tell me, how did you meet my son?"

"Well, I'm buying his house."

"Oh, yes, Evelyn did mention something of the sort. Thank goodness he's moving past that phase of his life. It's about time. Now that he's a partner, he'll need to get serious about his career. No more dabbling in that other stuff."

"He's actually quite talented at that other stuff."

Lillian raised one perfectly shaped eyebrow. Her superior air made Evelyn seem docile. "Let's get serious. He'll never amount to anything with that architecture foolishness. The Cains have been attorneys for generations. He has big shoes to fill and at last he seems to be doing an adequate job of that. There's absolutely no need to encourage him otherwise."

"Of course there is."

Her second eyebrow lifted and she eyed Nikki in surprise. "Excuse me?"

"Oh, Nikki, look, there's Nick. Did I ever introduce you?" Evelyn tugged on her arm.

Lillian gave her a scathing glare. "You can wait until we're finished with our conversation. If what you say is correct, then Nicole here—"

"It's Nikki."

Lillian's eyes narrowed on Nikki. "Nikki is a tramp's name. As long as you're dating my son, you'll be known as Nicole. I can't possibly introduce you to my friends otherwise."

"But I prefer Nikki. It is a perfectly acceptable name, just like architecture is a perfectly acceptable occupation."

"Look, missy, if you expect to rub shoulders with your social betters, you'll soon learn that your opinion is of little value around here."

Before Nikki could respond, a distinguished gentleman with salt-and-pepper hair interrupted. "Excuse me, dear, I couldn't help seeing you seem a little agitated." He eyed Nikki with a note of censure. "Is everything all right?"

"Nothing I can't handle, dear. Evelyn has brought us quite a little surprise is all."

Evelyn blushed as both gazes turned toward her. "N-Nikki, this is Mitchell Cain, Dylan's father. Mitchell, this is Nikki McClellan, Dylan's—"

"Latest conquest," Lillian finished for her as she cast a triumphant glance in Nikki's direction. "Girlfriend seems so benign and whore so crude, but I believe that's the gist of it. You do sleep with him, don't you, dear? I can't imagine why else he'd be interested. You've been with him for how long, and how many functions has he brought you to? At least he brought Kathy around to all the benefits and such, introduced her to his friends and family. Of course, he *loved* her. Probably still does, from the distress he suffered at her passing. No doubt he hasn't professed any such emotion in your case. Seems to me he's been keeping you to himself. He's relegated you to the bedroom, hasn't he, dear?"

Nikki stared at her, stunned. As far as she could tell, Dylan had done well to escape any mothering by this woman. The fact that Lillian seemed to be hitting a little too close to the truth only made her more vicious.

With great effort Nikki held her temper in check. She had to keep her head for Dylan's sake. "The thing is that it doesn't really matter what I am to your son. What matters is that I care about him very much. I respect and admire him as a human being and his happiness is of the utmost importance to me."

Evelyn twisted the huge diamond on her finger. "If

you'll excuse me, I think Nick needs me." She quickly melted into the crowd.

Mitchell straightened, his gaze narrowed on Nikki. "Surely you're not implying that we have anything but his best interest in mind."

She glanced through the crowd for Evelyn. She should go after the woman, make sure she wasn't up to something. But Nikki had to try to get through to Dylan's father first. She turned to him. "I certainly hope you do, sir. Are you aware that he's not satisfied practicing law in your firm?"

"Nonsense. He's just won his first big case. I was sure the media was going to crucify him, but he stuck to his guns and he pulled through."

"He can't even bring himself to talk about the case. If it was such a great success, why isn't he celebrating? Why isn't he retelling the story to everyone who'll listen?"

Lillian laughed a short little laugh filled with contempt. "Why, of course he's celebrating. That's what tonight is all about. Maybe he's just not talking to you about it. I'm sure the two of you spend your time in other pursuits that don't require conversation."

"You can try to belittle me as much as you want. It doesn't change the fact that you only see the Dylan you want to. You're not willing to see him for who he really is."

"And who would that be?" Mitchell asked.

"He has a creative soul that is stifling in that practice."

"Hogwash," Mitchell said. "Listen to me, young lady.

You will drop this nonsense once and for all. If you want to remain a part of our son's life, then you need to learn to play the game. Here are the rules. You will not encourage him to pursue an alternate career. You will not feed him any nonsense about leaving the firm. You will not provide him any advice about anything at all. Is that clear?"

Anger burned through Nikki. She looked at the closed faces around her. Dylan was so much better off without them. And so was she. "Abundantly clear."

"Good." Mitchell nodded to Lillian. "Now, if you'll excuse us. I see someone I need to speak with, then I'd like to toast my son's decision to follow in the family footsteps."

DYLAN GRITTED HIS TEETH and counted silently to ten as Baxter Jones belted out another of his embellishments on his latest courtroom success. How a judge and jury could sit through the man's long monologues was a mystery.

"Anyway, son, you remind me of myself back in the day. I told your father you'd do it. Never had a doubt." Baxter wound down and blinked at his empty glass.

"Why don't I find you a fresh one?"

Baxter brightened. "That would be rather good of you. Thanks."

Dylan took his glass and nodded, a smile plastered across his face. He dropped the glass on the first tray he saw and kept walking. If he had to suffer through another encounter with one of his father's cronies, he'd have to beat something. He was a moment away from telling them all exactly what he thought of their pretentious little world. Satisfaction filled him at the thought. What would it be like to leave all this behind?

To leave it behind and lose himself in his secret paradise with Nikki? Was there any reason why they couldn't spend more time with each other—possibly live together?

The thought of waking with her every morning sent a thrill of excitement through him. What would it be like to fall asleep each night with her in his arms, then awaken to her sweet smile?

"You're looking smart tonight." A whiff of heavy perfume drifted around him. Evelyn slipped her arm through his. "How does it feel to be the star of the show?"

"You know, I was just thinking that maybe this isn't quite the show I'd like to star in."

"That's a good one. You've worked all your life to get to this night." She gripped his arm and gestured to the clusters of people littering the ballroom of the antebellum mansion. "Look. They're the cream of the crop. Senators, diplomats, deal makers and deal breakers. And they are all here to celebrate *your* victory, not just in the courtroom but in your fight to make it into their ranks."

Her eyes shone as she turned to him. "You're playing with the big boys now, Dylan. You've made it."

"Right." So why did he still feel so empty?

"Kathy would be so proud of you."

"Would she?"

"Of course. This is what she wanted for you. What you both wanted."

He glanced around, and several people nodded or saluted him with sparkling champagne glasses. Empty people with empty lives. Why had he wanted this so badly?

The clinking of a crystal glass rang over the sound system. "Excuse me, everyone." His father's voice boomed across the room.

The chatter around them settled into murmurs, then faded to silence as the revelers turned their attention to the podium at the front of the spacious ballroom his mother had undoubtedly agonized for days over before renting.

Dylan straightened. What was Nikki doing now? What would she think of him dressed in this monkey suit, rubbing elbows with Miami's elite crowd?

"You all know why we're here tonight." His father puffed out his chest and beamed. "My dear wife, Lillian, and I have asked you here to help us toast our son."

He raised his glass. People from all around turned toward Dylan, their glasses raised high, their lips curved into gracious smiles. If he wasn't his father's son, would any of these people care about him? Would any of them bring him their cases if he weren't with Cain, Reynolds and Associates?

What a farce. They'd all shown their true colors when his parents had shunned his interest in architecture.

What had made him think any of them could see past his name now?

He stood stiffly while his father continued to speak. "We're here to celebrate a great victory. One of our finest citizens was charged with a grievous offense, but thanks to the efforts of our beloved son, Dylan—the newest partner at Cain, Reynolds, Cain and Associates—justice has again been served."

His father drank from his glass to a chorus of cheers and accolades. The crowd closed in around Dylan, a sea of nameless faces, each one trying to outdo the other with a brighter smile, more gracious words of praise. Someone slapped him on the back. An elderly matron bent in close to air-kiss his cheek, her ample bosom momentarily engulfing his upper arm.

He nodded back, his smile forced as he tamped down on the rising need to escape, to breathe fresh, clean air.

To see Nikki.

The matron shifted. "You are the spitting image of your father at your age. How I remember those days. What a charmer he was."

Dylan bobbed his head, focusing on a spot beyond her. A glimpse of rich brown hair flashed across his line of vision. His heart quickened and he strained to see through the crowd. No, of course Nikki wouldn't be there. This was the last place she'd be. What was he thinking?

"Why, look, there's Nikki." Evelyn somehow still hovered near his elbow in spite of the press of bodies around them.

"No." Nikki didn't belong here. She'd be like a helpless angelfish among sharks.

"Oh, but it is her."

He leaned around the bulk of the older woman. The brunette turned. His heart skipped a beat. He'd memorized that same shoulder, kissed a path across its soft skin. He stood rooted in place for one horrified moment.

Nikki was here.

His blood ran cold. She faced his parents. By his mother's outraged expression, his father's look of disgust and the straight line of Nikki's spine, things were not going well.

A confused mix of anger and fear raced through him. He had to get to her. He pushed through the crowd, brushing by one startled face after another. His gaze fixed on Nikki, whose back grew stiffer even as the color in his mother's face deepened and the bluster in his father's eyes intensified.

Mitchell Cain's voice vibrated with outrage as Dylan neared. "We've already had this conversation, miss. You're in over your head. I suggest you take your opinions and walk out of this ballroom and out of our son's life."

Nikki lifted her chin high. "Fine, I'll leave here, but I'll leave Dylan's life if, and only if, he wishes it."

"I wish it." The words flew from his mouth before he'd formed them in his mind.

Nikki whirled toward him, her eyes round with shock. "Dylan."

"You shouldn't have come tonight. You don't belong here." Why hadn't he stayed home with her? None of this would have happened. A sick feeling swirled in his stomach just to see her in the midst of these people.

His people.

"Dylan—" Nikki reached toward him, but he flinched away.

He was poison to her, just like the rest of them. The need to protect her—to send her from this den of lions—rose with a sharp ache. "Just go."

Pain flickered in her eyes. She lifted herself taller, then walked away. He closed his eyes against the sight of her departure. It was just as well they end things now. How could he have thought he could keep her isolated from the rest of his life?

13

DYLAN'S FATHER CLASPED his hands together in a gesture of thanks while his mother moved to embrace her son. "Thank God you're seeing things clearly. We set her straight once, but she came back for more. What nerve. That girl was no match for you."

Dylan held up his hand to stave her off. "You're wrong. *I'm* no match for her."

"Nonsense. She was lucky to have had her shot, but she's blown it. You've done the right thing," his father said.

"Tell me, what about her bothered you? Her directness? Her honesty—"

"Now, son—"

"Or was it just that she embarrassed you in front of your friends by breaking those fake smiles and drawing out the real you for all to see?"

"Well." Lillian drew herself up. "She's not exactly bringing out *your* best, is she?"

He pulled a breath deep into his lungs. Nikki must have really shaken them up for them to make such a public display. How could he have needed their acceptance—their love—so much? "You have no idea. There *was* no best in me before her."

"You're talking garbage." His father shook his finger at him.

It was all Dylan could do not to smack the offending digit away. How many times in his life had his father uttered that accusation? Well, he wasn't listening anymore. "For once, I don't think so."

"Then she's warped your thinking," his mother said. "If only you'd taken more interest in Evelyn. There's a girl for you. She understands the plan. She'd never lead you astray."

"Let's talk about this plan for a minute." He paused to make sure they were both listening. "From now on, the plan is to figure out what I really want to do with my life."

"That's ridiculous." Lillian's laugh lacked the conviction she no doubt meant to convey. "You already know what you want. You've just made partner. It's what you were born to do. It's what you've always wanted."

"Maybe I've decided that I don't want to keep using technicalities to set criminals loose on our streets."

Mitchell cringed and glanced around to see who might have heard. "What the hell are you talking about? How much have you had to drink?"

"Not nearly enough." With a shake of his head Dylan turned to leave.

"Young man, you get back here and explain yourself." The bark in his father's voice no longer carried the bite it had in the past, but Dylan stopped and faced the couple.

"Then let me make this abundantly clear. I quit." His parents' shocked expressions burned into his memory as he walked away.

DYLAN STARED AT NIKKI AS he reached the wide steps leading up to the mansion. She hadn't left as he had hoped. His heart pounded with irrational fear. He focused instead on his anger, stoking it with the knowledge that, had he not intervened, she would have been headed for disaster of the monumental kind.

Few people took on his parents directly without suffering some horrendous consequence. How many lives had they destroyed? Nikki had no idea how ruthless they were. She'd never seen them build up people, just to tear them down. She couldn't possibly comprehend the danger in which she'd just placed herself.

"Look…" She shifted from foot to foot. "I know you're upset. I may have overstepped my boundaries by coming here."

He held up his hand for her to stop. Still, it took him a moment to control the tidal wave of emotion crashing down on him before he could speak. "This place, these people—my people—they're not for you. You had no right to come here tonight."

"But, Dylan, I care about you and I want to help you."

"Help me?" He stared at her, incredulous. "How exactly does your showing up here help me?"

She seemed to lose some of her steam. "I needed to look out for you, to meet your people, to learn more about you."

"You know all you need to know." He paced a few steps away, then pivoted. "We had a deal. No frills. That means no more personal stuff than I am willing to share."

The spark lit in her eyes again. "Well, the hell with that deal. It was a stupid deal." She paused. "I'm sorry if I upset you by showing up, but I'm not sorry I came. I understand now a little more about why you're the way you are. I thank God for Kathy. I think without her you never would have known love. She taught you how to care about people. You sure didn't get that from those icebergs you call parents."

He stood still and let her rave. His own legs seemed barely able to hold him upright. Kathy may have understood, but she had never spoken the brutal truth of his life.

His parents had never loved him.

All these years he'd been chasing a dream with them. It was almost more than he could bear. He stared, unblinking, as Nikki's eyes filled with tears.

"They don't know the meaning of the word *love,* Dylan. How they could miss all the wonders you have to offer this world is beyond me." She stepped closer and laid her hand on his arm. "I'm so sorry for all the harm they've inflicted on you. I'm so sorry they don't have it in their little rock hearts to love you the way you deserve to be loved."

His hands fisted as he shielded himself from the truth. "It isn't your place to apologize for them."

She swiped her hand across her cheek. "They're a lost cause. There's no pleasing them. If you continue to try, you'll just keep disappointing them. That—" she gestured toward the house behind them "—gala may seem like pride from the outside, but I'd bet my last dime that's all for show."

"You should leave now."

Her expression crumbled, but she lifted her chin. "If that's really what you want."

He filled his gaze with the sight of her. She had discovered the lie of his life. "It's what I really want. You were wrong to come here."

She nodded and for the briefest moment he almost hoped that she might argue, but then, for the final time, she turned and walked away.

NIKKI SLAMMED HER CAR INTO park and swore. How could she have been so stupid? She'd played right into Evelyn's hands. Nikki had known the risk and she'd gone anyway. She should never have gotten her hopes up that way. Some help she'd been to Dylan.

She dropped her head to the steering wheel and cried. She'd screwed everything up. Ruined her chances with him. Destroyed any last shot at truly healing him.

She shuddered as the memory of her conversations with his parents came back to her. There was so little warmth in either of them. No wonder Dylan was so

closed off. They didn't care what was right for him—
for his happiness. All they saw was how they might
gain from his work at the firm, how it would look for
their star child to abandon the family profession and do
something so irresponsible as studying architecture.

Her anger rose and she straightened. Dylan had been
mad when he'd broken things off with her, but there had
been something else. When he'd approached her and his
parents, his fear had hit her in a wave. But what had he
feared? Did he fear his own parents? No, that didn't
seem right.

He must have been afraid for her.

Why would that be? Surely they wouldn't harm her
in any way. Yet his alarm had been almost palpable.

Had something happened between Kathy and his
parents?

She had to talk to Steven. She pulled his card from
her purse, staring at the embossed letters in the faint
light from a nearby streetlight. At this point it didn't
matter what Dylan thought about her fraternizing with
his friends. He couldn't get any more upset with her.

But maybe Steven could help her figure out why
Dylan had been so disturbed.

"YOU MUST BE NIKKI. COME in." A petite brunette who
could only be Steven's wife, Rebecca, ushered her into
a crowded foyer.

"Thank you."

"Don't mind all this." The woman gestured to a

bench overflowing with clothes and a stack of bulging cartons. "Dylan inspired us. We're cleaning out closets and giving away everything that we don't use anymore."

Nikki nodded. A vision of Dylan's master bedroom and its closet still filled with Kathy's clothes drifted through her mind. He may have been ready to lose the furniture and decorations, but he hadn't quite gotten around to parting with Kathy's most personal possessions.

"I'm Rebecca Benson. I'm so happy to meet you. I would have been at the gala but my mother was ill."

"I hope she's well now."

"She's fine. Nothing that a good antibiotic and some pampering won't take care of. Now, what can I get you to drink?"

"Oh, what are you having?"

"Strawberry iced tea."

"Sounds wonderful."

Rebecca led her to a brightly lit kitchen. Life-size sunflowers were painted on one wall. The scent of roasting herbs and spices drifted in the air.

"Have a seat." Rebecca nodded toward the large oak table with mismatched chairs. "Steven just called. He's running a little late but should be here any moment."

"I hope I'm not keeping you from anything."

"Not at all. I'm glad to have you to myself for a few minutes."

Nikki smiled and took the glass Rebecca offered, sipping the sweet tea. "This is good."

"I'm so glad Dylan met you, Nikki. He deserves to

be happy and, from what I can tell, you've brought more than a little joy into his life."

"I'm not so sure about that."

"I heard about what happened at the party and I can't tell you how sorry I am."

"I probably shouldn't have gone."

"I hate those things myself. The Cains invite us from time to time, mostly because Steven and Dylan are so close. But otherwise we don't really have an association with them."

"They do seem an elite group."

Rebecca laughed. "That's one way of putting it." She leaned forward, her green eyes intense. "I never met Kathy, but I've heard stories from Steven. You know, the three of them practically grew up together." She gazed out the garden window over the sink. "I wonder what would have become of Dylan without Steven…without Kathy."

"Rebecca, do you know anything about her relationship with Dylan's parents?"

"That I do know a little of. They never approved of her. She wasn't 'elite' enough for them. Came from the wrong bloodline, I guess."

"I got a taste of the way they treated Dylan the other night. I can only imagine how hard it must have been for her."

"She was a trooper, though." Steven stepped into the room. "So sorry for keeping you waiting. I see my dear wife has occupied you."

"She's been very hospitable."

"Hi, honey." Rebecca tilted her face up as Steven planted a kiss on her lips. "You were right. She's absolutely lovely."

"Our Dylan has always had the best taste in women. Only the cream of the crop for him." He squeezed Rebecca's shoulders and the warmth between the two flowed outward toward Nikki. "He's following my example."

He sat in a chair beside Rebecca and she leaned in toward him. "We were talking about Kathy and Dylan's parents."

"She had a lot of tolerance for them. For years she stood up to them, even though they snubbed her at every opportunity." He shook his head. "I don't know why he didn't just wash his hands of them years ago."

"Their approval has always been so important to him." Rebecca frowned. "But he stuck to his guns with Kathy."

"He insisted on bringing her with him to every function they attended. I suppose he hoped to wear them down eventually—that they'd get to know her and at least accept her." Steven rubbed a spot on the table. "I don't think he understood how low they were willing to stoop."

He paused a long while as he gazed into the distance. "The night of the accident Dylan had passed the bar and they—Mitch and Lillian—threw him a big party, of course." He focused on Nikki and sorrow and sympathy swirled in his eyes. His love for Dylan and

Kathy was vibrant and sad at once. "Dylan and Kathy were going to announce their engagement. Lillian caught wind of it, though. My guess is that Kathy had confided in Evelyn." He shrugged. "Evelyn has always been the daughter Lillian never had. It isn't hard to figure that Evelyn had told her."

Nikki leaned forward. "Steven, what happened that night?"

He glanced at Rebecca, who patted his hand, then back at Nikki. "I don't know all the details. Dylan has never spoken of it, but I can tell you what I pieced together.

"It was storming so bad, I thought they might call off the party. Unfortunately they didn't. I was there, toasting Dylan, just like the other night. Same faces, same stories. I hate those things. Only went for Dylan…and Kathy. She hated them even more than I did." The kitchen light shone in his hair as he shook his head. "It was like each time she was on trial…and found lacking. She put up a strong front for Dylan."

"They couldn't appreciate her, could they?" Nikki asked softly, her heart going out to the beautiful blonde in Dylan's photographs.

"No, and it seemed the harder he tried to force her on them, the worse it got. I guess it all came to a head that night. I didn't find out until later that Dylan had finally gotten up the nerve to ask Kathy to marry him. It should have been a happy time for them."

He was quiet for a moment, lost in thought. Then he continued his story. "I saw it from across the room. It was pretty crowded and the storm was blasting away. Lillian and Mitchell had Kathy cornered. It was impossible to hear from that distance, but any one could see how upset she was. My guess is they made some attempt to run her off before Dylan announced the engagement."

Whatever was roasting in the oven hissed and crackled. Rebecca went to turn down the heat, then refill the glasses. Steven waited until she was again seated. "All I know is that whatever they said upset her enough that she went tearing out of there in an awful hurry. She was crying. I could see that even though I was still too far away to stop her.

"Dylan ran after her, but he was too late. She took off in the rain without waiting for the valet. The storm had gotten even worse, with thunder booming and lightning streaking all across the sky. It was a horrible, horrible night. She must have had an extra set of keys, because I could hear her tires squealing by the time I hit the front steps. Dylan was already racing down the driveway after her."

He shook his head. "She lost control around the first bend. I still remember the sound of it—her tires locking, that…boom…when she hit the power pole." He stopped.

Rebecca covered his hand with hers. "I'm so sorry, Steven. I know in your own way you loved her, too."

He nodded. "Dylan hasn't been the same ever since."

Nikki closed her eyes and let out her breath. At least now she knew. "He's blamed them all this time, hasn't he?"

A frown marked Steven's brow. "You mean, Lillian and Mitchell?"

"Yes, he blames them for her death."

Steven considered for a moment. "I guess I never thought of it that way, but, yes, I think you could be right. You know, he quit the firm."

"No, I didn't know." At least there was that. Maybe now he'd move on with his life.

"The other night at the gala…after you…left."

"Well…" She pushed away from the table. "Thank you for sharing Kathy's story with me."

"What will you do now?" Rebecca asked.

"I'm not sure. He opened such a small part of his life to me and I forced my way into the rest. Now I have to face the consequences." She heaved a sigh. "It's over between us. He made that clear the other night."

"But, Nikki, wait. Don't you see?" Steven reached for her.

"See what?"

"He blamed his family for Kathy's death. So he kept you away from them. In some odd, irrational way, he was protecting you."

"But why? They didn't pose any threat to me."

"Why else? He did it because he cares for you— probably more than he even realizes. No doubt it scared the hell out of him to see you there reenacting the scene with them."

She paused a long moment. Could Steven be right?

Had Dylan purposely kept her from his family in order to protect her from them? "So what should I do?"

Steven's gaze grew intense. "Do you care for him? Really care for him?"

"Yes."

"Then don't give up on him, Nikki. You've got to give him another chance."

She nodded slowly. Maybe Steven was right. But how would she convince Dylan to take that chance?

14

NIKKI TURNED THE KNOB ON Sophie's front door and sighed. No matter the troubles weighing her, arriving on her aunt's doorstep always seemed to lighten them. Sophie would have the answers. She'd know exactly what to say to help Nikki find her way through this fiasco with Dylan.

She pushed the door open and breathed in the aromatic scent of herbs hanging from the ceiling of Sophie's entryway.

Yes, she felt better already.

The soft clink of dishes in the kitchen drew her. What was Sophie brewing now? A tonic to quiet a cough? Special tea to calm one's worries? Soup to soothe the soul?

Nikki followed the sounds, stopping just inside the arched entry. Sunlight dipped through the parted curtains over the large porcelain sink. There, glancing up in surprise, a bottle of vodka in her hand, stood Maggie.

A smile spread across her face, and for just an instant Nikki could believe her mother was actually pleased to see her. She paused, uncomfortable to be caught alone with Maggie so unexpectedly. Old anger and resentment rose in her, mixing with a newfound curiosity.

"Nikki." Maggie motioned with the bottle. "I was just fixing myself a screwdriver. Would you like one?"

"Sophie's not here?"

Her mother's lips thinned a fraction and something that might have been hurt registered briefly in her eyes before she smiled and finished pouring her drink. "No, she had a date."

"A date?"

"Uh-huh, with a rather dashing gentleman, I must say."

So no tea, no soup. Just Maggie and vodka. Well, Maggie always had been nothing if not unexpected.

Nikki's gaze fell to the two glasses on the table. "Were you expecting someone?"

A small smile played across her mother's lips. "I just had a feeling. Join me?"

Nikki hesitated a long moment before moving to the table. "Sure."

"Take a seat." Maggie handed her the drink, then sat in one of the big oak chairs that had held at least two generations of McClellan women.

"Thomas had a feeling we'd be seeing you. Why didn't you call and let us know you were coming?"

"I was going to call you girls as soon as I caught my breath. I got in this afternoon."

"If you're tired I can go."

"The jet lag hasn't set in yet. I'll get a good night's sleep tonight and be fine tomorrow."

"You do always seem to bounce back." In fact, as Nikki thought about it, it seemed her mother had lived an unusually healthy life. And she'd kept her youthful demeanor. She'd been mistaken for the girls' sister on more than one occasion. Did this have anything to do with the McClellan gift?

Maggie took a long swallow of her drink, then set down her glass. She cocked her head at Nikki. "So how are you? Everything still going well at the clinic?"

"Oh, yeah, great."

"But something's not right."

Of course she wouldn't be able to hide anything from her mother. "I've been better."

Maggie's forehead puckered for a moment, then she nodded. "It's a man, isn't it?"

"Why didn't you tell us?"

"Tell you what?"

Nikki gestured with her glass. "About the McClellan heritage—our…gift."

Her mother gazed at her as if she were trying to comprehend the question.

"You could have mentioned that we were…special."

"Ah, sweetheart, weren't you with me through all those years?"

"Well, yes, but—"

"Why did I need to explain what you could see with your own eyes?"

"But you have to understand that we…may not have interpreted what was happening quite the way you might have wanted us to."

"Those who aren't ready to see can't be made to see."

"You could have tried."

"Would you have listened?"

Nikki paused. Her family legacy had been hard enough to hear coming from Sophie. Would she have heard the truth from Maggie?

"I don't know."

Maggie sat straight in her chair. "I make no excuses for the way I have lived my life or for how I've raised you girls. You have each grown to be beautiful, successful, self-reliant individuals. I am exceedingly proud of all of you. There isn't a thing I'd change. Would you?"

Nikki stared at her mother for a long moment. Was her independence and current success in life worth the sacrifice of a loving relationship with her mother? "I'm not sure."

Disappointment flickered in Maggie's eyes. She drank deeply from the glass. "So you've fallen in love."

Nikki swallowed past the tightening in her throat. She hadn't meant to cause her mother any grief. "Is it so obvious? I've only just figured it out myself."

"I feared this for you. Not the falling in love part, that's a given. But the thing you're having trouble with is the letting go. Isn't it?"

Nikki nodded. "Thomas says you fall in love every time."

"I do." She frowned. "How else?"

"But…none of it is meant to last. How can you let yourself love someone if you know you have to let them go?"

"A sunset doesn't last, yet its beauty is intricately tied to its transience," Maggie explained.

"How? How do you let go when it's time?"

"When it's time, then letting go is the most natural thing in the world."

"Doesn't it hurt?"

"Nikki, do you remember when you were eight and you and Tess found that bird with the bent wing?"

Nikki gestured impatiently. "And Sophie helped us nurse it back to health and, yes, it was wonderful letting it go and watching it fly away. But you can't compare my relationships with men to healing that bird."

"You loved the bird."

Nikki stared at her in exasperation. "Yes, I loved the bird, but not in the same way."

"Exactly." Maggie sat back, smiling as though they'd solved everything.

"Why am I bothering?" Nikki pushed away from the table. She should have known better than to solicit advice from her mother.

"Just like loving the bird was different, so is the letting go."

Nikki paused. The memory of Dylan, his face deadly calm, the darkness of his despair shrouding him, seeping out to cut through her like a million knives. The room blurred. "But he ended it and he was in so much pain."

"Oh, my…a wounded soul."

"There was nothing natural or beautiful about it."

Tears streamed down Nikki's cheeks. She swiped at them, horrified to be falling apart in front of her mother. Never, not since she'd been a very young child, had she let Maggie see her cry.

"But don't you see? The time wasn't right. He fights the healing."

"So what do you do with a man who insists on living with his ghosts?"

"I'd say you haven't much choice." She shook her head. "I have never encountered this, so it's hard to say, but it seems his wounds run deep. Either this is part of his life lesson—not to heal—or you'll need extra care to heal him."

"He doesn't want anything to do with me."

"For now, he may say that, but I'm betting a time will come when he will have to choose between continuing his suffering and joining the living."

"What if he's already made that choice?"

Maggie gripped her shoulder. "If you truly love him, you have to believe he'll choose life."

Nikki nodded. Was there still hope for Dylan?

"Then, when the time comes, you must be there, ready to love him heart and soul."

"And how do I face each day until then?"

"That part is easy. You hone your craft."

"What do you mean?"

"You have a gift. A master pianist might be gifted, but he studies and practices to increase his skill."

"I don't know how I feel about practicing our particular gift. To tell you the truth, I don't think I can be with anyone right now."

"But you can study tantric healing."

"Tantric healing? Is that what it's called?"

"That is one form of it. I have some books you can read. Search in your bookstore or online. You'll find the right resources for you."

"Will a book teach me how to let go?"

"I'm afraid that's something that may have to come with practice. I'm sorry, this has never been an issue with me. Perhaps the difficulty you're feeling revolves around the fact that he's resisted the healing." She sighed. "Give it some time. Maybe you're just trying too hard."

Nikki's frustration mounted. "Sophie said there are no hard and fast rules. That there's a norm, but individual experiences have varied from that."

"Yes…" Maggie's frown deepened. "It seems I've heard some stories." She focused on Nikki, her eyes filled with concern. "Tragedies, really."

"Has there…has there ever been an instance where someone found one great love?"

"You mean one great *lasting* love?"

"Yes, a lasting love, a true love, whatever you want to call it."

Silence ebbed around them as Maggie thought. At long last she sighed. "I'm not sure, honey. Maybe Sophie would know."

"I've had this conversation with Sophie. She certainly didn't have anything positive to say about it."

"I guess it could be possible. It's just contrary to the nature of the gift, since it would mean staying with this one love and not moving on to heal others."

Nikki nodded. Hope flickered through her. If it were possible that she could find one true love, then maybe she could bear losing Dylan.

Or maybe Dylan *was* that love.

"I'm sure there would be consequences, though," Maggie warned.

"Consequences for staying with one man, you mean?"

"Yes."

"What kind of consequences?"

The look of concern Maggie wore intensified. "I would think that staying with one man could well cost you your gift."

DYLAN YANKED ON A WEED and failed again in his latest attempt to force Nikki from his mind. The woman had him all twisted up inside. Just the thought of her touch brought a mixture of peace and despair. Peace in the memory of her…healing qualities. Despair in the sure knowledge that he'd driven her and her odd magic out of his life for good.

His gaze swerved from the clump of green in his hand to the barren clay pot beside the fountain. He scowled. Damn, he'd been a little exuberant in his weeding. He dropped the clump back into the pot and huffed out a breath. What the hell was wrong with him?

"Dylan, there you are." Evelyn's too-sweet voice sounded from behind him.

He turned. She stood with her back to the setting sun, her damn fiancé glued to her side.

"Dylan." Nick nodded a greeting.

"Nick." Dylan rose, brushed off the dirt, then briefly shook the man's hand.

Evelyn peered at him. "Dylan, what are you doing? And why are you doing it?"

"This, my dear, is called yard work. I'm tending to my garden."

"Looks more like you're desolating it." She indicated the planter around the fountain.

He glanced over his shoulder and cringed. The dark soil lay exposed and broken. Only fragments of the flowers remained. He had indeed been most efficient in his weeding. "I'm thinking I might start fresh with something new."

"But, darling, I know you have a service to take care of that. Why on earth are you bothering with it?" Evelyn wrinkled her nose in disgust.

"So is there a point to this little visit, or did I just get lucky?" He was being a prick, but somehow he couldn't stop himself.

Nick clasped Evelyn's hand. "Evelyn wanted to drop in and see how you're doing."

"We were in the neighborhood house hunting," she hurried to add. "Isn't that exciting? We might be neighbors."

Not likely, since he was moving soon. And thank God because he couldn't stand little visits like this all the time. His irritation built, filling him until he nearly burst with it. "So you came to check up on me. What's the matter—my sweet mother afraid I've gone off to dirty the family name?"

Evelyn's eyes widened. "If I *was* here at your mother's request, what would be so wrong with her wanting to check to see that her only child was faring okay after that horrendous scene at the party?"

"Tell me something, Evelyn. When are you going to wise up and quit brownnosing my parents?"

"I don't think that's called for." Nick draped his arm protectively around her shoulders as she pulled herself up as straight as a pole.

"That is so unfair. Maybe I needed to know for myself that you were okay."

"Well, if you're so concerned for my welfare, why didn't you think about that before you invited Nikki to that party?"

She stared at him openmouthed.

"Come on, Evelyn, who else? I told you to stay away from her. You knew I didn't want her sucked into that slime pit of a family I have—"

"That is a horrible thing to say about your parents—"

"You just had to interfere. I thought I saw your car the day of the yard sale. What did you do? Wait around for the opportunity to talk to her when I wasn't here? Did you see me leave, then decide to make your appearance?"

Her face turned scarlet. "We may have stopped by, but I can't recall if you were here."

"Look, honey, he's obviously fine. Let's go." Nick took her arm to lead her away.

Evelyn made a feeble protest but let Nick guide her through the archway toward his Jag parked prominently in the drive. She glanced back once, but when Dylan glared, she tossed her head and continued on.

He stood, feet planted and hands fisted, until long after they'd gone and the last of the sun's rays drifted below the horizon. The fading light seemed to drain him of his guilt, of his anger, of his strength. He was empty, a hollow shell, ready to be crushed and broken against the fates. He stumbled to the hammock and fell into it, too tired to even make it into the house.

The fountain splashed and gurgled. A flock of birds flew by. He breathed in the sweet aroma of summer flowers and for the briefest moment let himself be transported to that first time with Nikki, when she'd brought him to such indescribable ecstasy.

Nikki.

She was as mysterious and magical as one of Kathy's mermaids. The two would have been great friends. He could feel it in his gut, Kathy's whimsical nature lightening Nikki's intensity and Nikki stabilizing Kathy. They were different but made of the same strong cloth.

And he'd lost them both.

He closed his eyes. As the darkness closed in around him, he imagined Nikki beside him.

Fight, Dylan. Fight the darkness, she seemed to whisper with the wind.

He clenched his fist on the empty spot beside him. He'd been right when he'd told his parents he was no match for her. Nikki walked her true path.

Maybe it was time he walked his.

15

DYLAN'S GAZE SWERVED FROM the cluster of eighteen-and nineteen-year-olds gathered in the hall outside the admissions office to the class enrollment form in his hand. The knot in his gut tightened, anxiety over starting again at this late date filling him.

He'd been excited when American InterContinental University had accepted him, giving him credit for his past courses and real-life experience. He'd armed himself with the determination of a man who'd walked away from one life and had embarked on a new one. He'd brought the admissions director a portfolio filled with small projects he'd helped Steven with over the years, as well as all the notes and drafts on his house. The man had been duly impressed. He'd even let Dylan enroll right away. He was able to audit courses, though the summer session was well under way.

Now all he had to do was choose some classes. Ignoring the students milling about, he glanced over the list in front of him: Architectural Drafting, Engineering Graphics, Materials and Processes. He swallowed as doubt assailed him. It had been so long since he'd sat in a classroom, completed term assignments or crammed for exams.

Everyone deserves happiness, Dylan.

Nikki's words drifted back to him and his resolve hardened. He'd spent too long in the gloom. If he ever hoped to find happiness, he had to start with himself.

One thing he knew for sure: practicing law had *not* made him happy. It made him sick to think of the number of guilty clients he'd helped walk through some technicality. He'd been good at his work, no doubt. But facing himself in the mirror each morning had gotten more difficult with each day.

No more.

He lifted his pen and bent over the page. "Materials and Processes, here I come."

Moments later he glanced over the completed form, a sense of accomplishment filling him. He'd pull a full load and spend as much time shadowing Steven as possible. Suddenly his future looked brighter. He had nothing to offer right now, but if he actually saw this through, would he have a chance then with Nikki?

SQUELCHING INCESSANT thoughts of Dylan, Nikki trailed into her living room. Tess lay sprawled on the lounger while Ramon painted her toenails and Nash, another of her minions, sat in a nearby chair sketching them in what appeared to be charcoal.

"What are you doing?" Nikki asked Tess.

Tess glanced up from the book in her lap. "I'm reading. It's most fascinating stuff."

She raised the book and Nikki read the title. *"Tantric Healing for Beginners."*

"You should read it," Tess said. "I have all kinds of new exercises to try. Ramon is my victim."

"Always willing for you, my sweet." He blew gently on her toes, then moved on to her other foot.

"What kinds of exercises?"

"Well, the first has to do with a chakra cleansing."

"A what?"

"I know about those." Nash glanced up from his drawing. "They're energy centers."

"Energy whats?"

"Yeah." Tess sat up straighter. "Little swirling things. Here's a picture."

She flipped through the book, then held the open page toward Nikki. Nikki moved closer and squinted at a photograph of a woman with a rainbow of circles overlaid along the vertical axis of her body. "Hey, I think I've seen those."

"You can see them?" Nash asked, and Tess looked questioningly at her.

Nikki blushed. "Sometimes when I'm, uh, when I'm with a man…you know, and we're, um…"

"When you're doing it, you see chakras?" Tess asked.

Nash focused on Nikki, as if he were trying to see the colored wheels of energy. He flipped to a new page, then started sketching with broad strokes.

"Well, maybe not exactly like that, but I kind of feel this rainbow race up my spine and it bursts…" She gestured above her head with her hands, stopping as they all stared at her. "It's just always been like that. I thought it was normal. I never really understood what it was. It's good to know I'm not nuts after all. I'd like to learn about these—what did you call them?"

Tess consulted her book. "Chakras. I haven't quite gotten them down. Something like main intersections of the meridians used in acupuncture. It's all new to me. You can read this when I'm done, though."

"I can help." Maggie moved into the room from behind Nikki.

Nikki turned, surprised. "I didn't know you were here."

"I've been in with Erin."

"Is she okay?" Tess asked with a note of concern. "She's been keeping to herself even more since her thing the other week with Ryan, who, by the way, wasn't looking too chipper when he left. Don't know what happened with those two, but she refuses to talk about it."

"Ryan—was that the young man's name? No, I guess that didn't quite work out the way she'd anticipated. I was hoping I could talk to her, but she's not open to hearing anything I have to say."

Tess made a short sound of derision. "Join the club. We thought setting her up would perk her up, but that didn't work. And even though she doesn't know we had a hand in it, somehow I know she's blaming us for this latest disaster."

"She's going through an adjustment period." Maggie shrugged. "I think we should let her ripen. She'll be fine."

"Ripen?" Nikki asked. "You sound like Sophie."

"Well, dear, Erin's young yet."

"I'm going to talk to her." Nikki turned toward the hall, but Maggie touched her arm.

"Wait, sweetie. She's okay. Just needs a little time to herself. She's going to join us for dinner later."

"Are you sure?"

"Trust me."

Nikki assessed her mother. Maggie had been a lot of things to her in the past—a never-ending embarrassment, the cause of all her troubles, the bane of her existence—but the one thing her mother had always been was honest. Sometimes painfully so. "Okay, I'll leave her alone. But if she isn't here for dinner, I'm going in after her."

"And I'll back you up." Maggie held her gaze for a moment and some of the tension drained from Nikki.

Her mother cocked her head. "Walk with me?"

For a long moment Nikki hesitated, resisting her initial impulse to blow off her mother. It seemed to have been a defense mechanism she'd developed growing up. More times than not, spending time with her mother brought news of an impending move. But that wasn't an issue any longer. Nikki was making her own home now.

She should at least give Maggie a chance. "It's pretty hot out there."

"It's late enough in the day, it's starting to cool. Come on, we'll walk along the beach, where the heat is less intense and we might catch a breeze."

"Hey, I'll come," Tess offered.

Maggie gave her a smile. "Can I take a rain check, Tess? I'd like some time with your sister."

"Sure, but I want to know about any tips on tantric healing you give her."

"Deal." Maggie turned to Nikki. "What do you say?"

"Okay." Nikki nodded. "I'll go."

"SEE THAT TREE?" MAGGIE nodded toward a palm tree in the distance as she and Nikki strolled along Central Miami Beach.

A warm breeze brushed the hair clinging to Nikki's neck. She nodded and sank her feet into the cool water ebbing and flowing along the shore.

"Trees are so wonderful. Their roots reach deep into the ground while their branches touch the sky. They take nourishment from the earth and light from the heavens. There's much we can learn from that."

"Like what?"

"Just like the tree, we join heaven and earth here in our bodies. Tantra helps us attune to nature—helps us expand our awareness through that attunement."

Nikki shook her head. "I don't see how that relates to lovemaking."

"If we understand the harmony in nature, we can better understand our bodies and our energy."

"Our energy? You mean those chakra things Tess talked about?"

"The chakras are like a map of the energy centers. When your chakras are open and balanced, the energy of the universe runs freely through you. Part of your gift is that when your heart chakra opens in love, it cues the rest of your chakras to open and balance. Your chakras in turn help balance and align your partner's. It comes naturally with the gift, but meditation can make it even stronger. There are even exercises you can do."

"So when these chakras are closed and the energy isn't flowing, this causes illness?"

Maggie nodded. "They can not only be closed, they can be open too wide or damaged. The energy can be clouded or blocked. All kinds of things go wrong when we don't follow spirit." She smiled. "Most of us need time to work our healing through each of the chakras, but you seem to get them all in one blast, so to speak."

"Or I did." She cocked her head. "Is it possible I've lost the gift?"

Her mother regarded her a long moment as they continued walking. "I wouldn't think so."

"But I didn't help him. I don't think I ever really got through to him."

"I'm sure you did in some way. It could be part of his path *not* to be healed." She slowed and turned to Nikki. "Or maybe you knocked at the wrong door?"

"You sound like Sophie. What does that mean?"

"In lovemaking and tantric healing you have to find the right door through the senses. Some people respond to visual stimulation, some auditory and some through touch and emotion."

"You're saying one of these senses is the key to his healing?"

Maggie shrugged. "I knew a man once who had a great breakthrough only when we made love in front of a huge mirror. It was the visual impact that helped him. He had to 'see' the love I offered before he could accept it. The key may be visual for your young man or it could be something else."

"I'll have to think about that. I've had some success getting him to open by talking, but I don't know. Maybe I should have tried something else. It doesn't really matter now. It's over."

"Maybe. But keep one thing in mind if you should see him again. You heal through the love, and the way to reach the love is to step past your fear."

Nikki nodded. Her fear of losing Dylan had most likely kept her from expressing her true feelings. "Well, I'll keep that in mind should I hear from him again, though I'm not holding my breath. I'm afraid Dylan Cain has moved out of my life and on with his own."

"YOU NEED SOME SERIOUS HELP. Do they always whine like that?" Dylan peered at the pair of red-faced toddlers Steven had just chased out of his neighborhood pool.

"I don't think so." Steven wrapped the first blond-haired girl in an oversize towel that would have tripped her up had he not been holding her.

Dylan corralled her equally blond sister as Becca attempted to catch her with a matching towel. "Come on, sweetie. Don't you want to dry off?"

"They just whine when they're tired or hungry or upset about something, right, Becca?" Steven asked her, his face intent as he unwrapped his squirming package, then tried to wrestle her into a pink ruffled cover-up that coordinated with her swimsuit.

"So my sister says." She tossed Dylan an apologetic glance. "I'm sorry. Mom was going to watch them, but she's still feeling a little under the weather. Steven and I thought for sure we could handle them for one afternoon."

"You said *you* could handle them. I made some noncommittal response that you took for agreement."

"There, see? Marital bliss as always." Rebecca beamed at her husband.

Having effectively garbed and distracted his young niece with a cookie, Steven swept his wife to his side and gave her a noisy kiss on her cheek. Niece number two—whose name and age had escaped Dylan in the flurry of the afternoon except that she was barely ten months younger than her sister—giggled and calmed long enough to snatch a second cookie from Steven's hand.

"I don't know about you two, but I'm exhausted just watching them. Where do they get all that energy?" Dylan helped Steven collect the assorted paraphernalia they'd hauled in with their charges: juice cups, sunscreen, matching hats that never managed to stay on their heads, a bag full of toys and water wings.

"Just watch. They'll be passed out by the time we get back to our house. With luck, they'll sleep until Peg picks them up at five," Steven said.

Niece number two obediently took Becca's hand as they all headed toward the parking lot. Her sister's head rested on her uncle's shoulder as he carried her to the car. Dylan loaded the various bags and a striped umbrella into the trunk while Steven and Becca buckled the youngsters into matching car seats.

Dylan stood back and dug through his pockets for his keys. Steven had trouble with the buckle and Becca leaned over to help him. On the whole, they formed quite a domestic picture. When Steven slipped his arm around his wife and they paused for a moment to gaze at their nieces, who were indeed settling down with drooping eyelids, an odd sensation stirred in the pit of Dylan's stomach.

In spite of the trouble the two young terrors had caused throughout the afternoon, in spite of the fact that they were someone else's children, his friends cared for them as if they were their own. Steven had mentioned that he and Rebecca were trying for their first. It wouldn't be long before they formed a happy family of their own.

Dylan cleared his throat. "Can you two make it from here on your own?"

"We've got it." Steven nodded, his arm still wrapped

around Becca. He motioned toward the backseat. "They look pretty harmless once they're asleep."

Dylan swallowed past a lump in his throat as his gaze flitted over the pink-cheeked faces. No sense getting too attached to the idea of sweet sleeping children. It wasn't as if there were any in his future. "Yeah, harmless."

Becca freed herself and moved beside him to plant a firm kiss on his cheek. "Thanks for helping out today. We probably weren't as ready as we thought."

"They're a handful."

"Well, we'll just start with one. Then we'll see."

"That sounds safe. You take care." He turned to Steven. "I'll see you tomorrow. I've got a drawing with the new foundation I want to show you."

"That's straight. I'll check it out. You have a good night. Hey, Dylan, have you thought any about calling Nikki?"

Dylan blew out a breath. That one had caught him off guard. "She'll be by next Saturday for the inspection. We'll see how that goes."

Becca frowned but refrained from comment. The look she gave him said it all, though: he was an idiot.

He bade them goodbye and headed for his car. If he'd had little to offer Nikki before, he had even less now. No partnership, minimal income for the next few years and not nearly enough time in the day.

How could he possibly call her?

As he pulled out of the lot and passed Steven's car, that odd sensation stirred again in Dylan's gut. Steven had it all: a thriving career, an adoring wife and the possibility of a family.

Could that odd feeling be envy? He shoved the unpleasant thought aside, along with the disturbing thought that Saturday and Nikki were just a few short days away.

16

A SLIGHT BREEZE STIRRED the thick afternoon air as Nikki stood on Dylan's doorstep with Ginger. The strange vehicle in the driveway seemed to indicate that the house inspector had already arrived.

She inhaled deeply to try to dispel the funny feeling in her stomach as footsteps approached from inside the house. Dylan opened the door, then stepped back to let them enter. "Come in. The inspector has been here for a little while. I hope you don't mind he's already started."

"He's the best," Ginger assured Nikki as she brushed past Dylan.

Nikki nodded and glanced toward Dylan, her heart thrumming. He avoided making eye contact with her and moved ahead of them into the kitchen. He gestured toward a man who fiddled with the lock on one of the windows. "Ladies, this is Hank Morris, the inspector."

"Morning." The elderly gentleman nodded, his expression serious.

"Hank and I go way back. Don't we, Hank?" Ginger patted her hair.

"Yes, ma'am."

Nikki cleared her throat. "So how does it look so far?"

Hank moved to the next window. "So far so good. The seal is going on that refrigerator, though."

Her gaze swerved to Dylan and he shrugged. For just that second, the awkwardness seemed to evaporate between them and it was as though the night of the gala had never taken place. "Well, I don't think that's a problem. As long as the house's structure is sound, I'm sure we can work out the rest of the details."

The inspector puckered his lips. "I just tell you like I see it. You make the call on what's acceptable."

"He'll give us a written report when he's done." Ginger gestured to the kitchen table. "Why don't we have a seat?"

"Yes…" Dylan hurried to pull out a chair for the agent. "Make yourselves comfortable."

"Thank you, dear." The chair creaked as Ginger settled into it. "What is this I hear about you quitting your daddy's firm? And right after making partner?"

This time he caught Nikki's eye as he held her chair. Warmth bloomed in her cheeks. She glanced away as she sat.

"Well, you heard right." He dropped into the chair opposite Nikki.

"Looks good in here." Hank made a note on his clipboard. "This way into the garage?"

Dylan nodded and the man left. Ginger leaned across the table. "So out with it. Whatever made you do such a thing? I just couldn't believe it, what with you getting the councilman acquitted and all. Seems to me you had it made."

His shoulders shifted beneath his golf shirt. Again his gaze pinned Nikki. "Just something I had to do."

Ginger's penciled-in eyebrows drew together. "But why? I don't understand it."

"I think what he's saying is that he wasn't happy practicing law."

"Oh." Ginger shook her head. "I'll bet that didn't make your folks too happy."

"You're right about that." He leaned back, seemingly at ease.

Ginger's eyes narrowed as she digested that piece of news, her frown deepening. "So now what are you going to do? Go to work for a competitive firm? I hear the D.A. is looking for someone."

The question had Nikki turning to him, as well. He blew out a breath, then grinned. "Nikki's right. I'm through with law. I'm studying architecture. One of the local colleges took pity on me and accepted my application for enrollment. I've been working with Steven Benson, a good friend of mine who's a local architect and who's letting me do a kind of apprenticeship with him. I'm doing that as well as taking classes."

"That's wonderful, Dylan," Nikki answered as Ginger squinted in an effort to absorb this new piece of information.

He grinned and confidence radiated off of him. "You were right about a lot of things, Nikki."

Ginger's gaze swept from one to the other, but her cell phone rang as she opened her mouth to comment. "I hope you two will excuse me. It seems you have plenty to talk about, and I would love to hear the details, but I have to take this call."

After she'd left, Nikki turned back to Dylan. "So things are going well for you?"

"Well enough. I'm already missing that hefty income, but I'll survive."

"Of course you will. I never doubted that for a moment."

His eyebrows drew together. "Funny, I did. I clung to that old life for all those years." His gaze pinned her. "I couldn't have made this change without you. I owe you thanks for at least that. I owe you an apology, too."

"For what?"

"It was wrong of me to take so much from you and give so little in return. I never deserved you."

She was quiet a moment. "You *have* given to me. You've given your time to me. You've given me pleasure. Everyone deserves happiness, Dylan. In this moment here with you, I'm happy just seeing you again. Aren't you?"

"I shouldn't be."

"And why not?"

"Maybe some of us don't deserve to be happy."

"I suppose my aunt would say some people come to

this earth to learn about unhappiness. But if that was your purpose, I'd say you've learned that lesson well and now it's time to let a little joy into your life."

He cocked his head. "You brought me joy."

She smiled. Both pleasure and pain shot through her. "I'll tell you something that might be hard to believe. It was my gift—to bring you healing through my touch."

He cocked his head. Curiosity mixed with his surprise. "Seriously?"

"I wish it weren't so."

"Why?"

"I was born into it. It wasn't my choice."

"Okay…" He leaned toward her. His acceptance was almost as ready as Tess's had been. It flowed out to her in a comforting wave. "So you *are* some kind of…enchantress. That's why I feel peace when I'm with you but the torment is tenfold when you're away. You *have* bewitched me."

"I'm not an enchantress. But I am a healer, and your resistance is what brings your torment."

"A healer? You heal with your touch?"

"Specifically through my lovemaking. Go ahead and laugh. It does sound ridiculous. I found it hard to believe myself. I still have my own issues with it."

"You mean sexual healing? I don't find it laughable at all. In fact, I'm not all that surprised. You *do* have a healing touch. I felt it when we first shook hands. I could feel your magic even then. I've felt it when I've been with you ever since." He blew out a breath. "Is that why I can't stay away from you?"

"As I understand it, when you resist the healing, it makes the parting hard."

He reached for her hand. "Nikki...I'm sorry."

"I'm fine." She shrugged. "You lasted the longest so far."

"There've been others? That you used your...healing on?"

"None like you." She cleared her throat and straightened. "So I've been studying, too."

"Have you?"

"Yeah, it's kind of strange, but my mother has been mentoring me on the family...heritage."

"It doesn't just come naturally?"

"Well, it does to some extent. The more I learn, the more I realize that many of the practices seem inherent—like I was born with some previous knowledge of them, but I don't remember it."

"That *is* a little strange." A teasing light shone in his eyes.

"You wouldn't believe the reading list she's assigned me."

He chuckled softly. "I'd like to see some of those books. So...no hands-on homework assignments?" Again his tone teased, but apprehension ran as an undercurrent to the question.

"No, there hasn't been anyone to practice all this new knowledge on."

He nodded and a stream of relief spiraled outward from him. Warmth filled her. He did still care about her. Maybe there was hope for them yet.

"Nikki?" Ginger reappeared in the doorway. "I'm so sorry, sweetie, but would you mind if we got together later to go over Hank's report? I have a slight emergency I need to take care of."

"Oh, no, not at all. You take care of whatever you need to. We'll tie this up later when you have a chance."

"You're an angel. Isn't she, Dylan?" She threw him a speculative glance. "Do you want me to drop you at home, Nikki? I'd forgotten you rode with me."

"I'll see that she gets home."

Nikki's pulse raced as Dylan's gaze locked with hers. Ginger thanked him, then bade them goodbye with the promise to call Nikki later. All the while, Nikki drank in the desire that flowed from Dylan in soft waves. This was not the fierce hunger she'd felt from him in the past. The intensity of it had curbed, transforming it into more of an uncertain longing.

Her eyes misted and she rose to put some distance between them. Footsteps sounded in the hall and the house inspector peered in at them. "That's it. I'll write up my report, then get it to Mrs. Parker. You'll have a copy, too, Mr. Cain."

"That'll be fine. Thank you." Dylan shook his hand and Nikki nodded from her spot by the sink.

She stood rooted in place, even after the scrape of the front door opening then closing drifted to them from down the hall. Distant sounds of traffic filtered from outside. The warmth of the sun penetrated the glass of the window and melted into her skin, sending gooseflesh rippling up her arms.

Dylan moved to stand beside her. He ran his hand up her arm, smoothing away the bumps. "Nikki, I…"

She cupped his cheek. "It's okay."

"No, it isn't. Nothing's quite okay without you. I…miss you."

Then she was in his arms and his mouth claimed hers. The kiss only fed the longing as they maneuvered closer, tongues dueling, bodies straining. Her heart thrummed as he lifted her and carried her to his bed.

Dylan broke the kiss to lay Nikki on the soft comforter, then he stretched out beside her. "I'd like to offer a new deal."

"No deals, Dylan. Not this time."

"But I want more. You've helped me see that I shouldn't have shut you out before—that I should have shared more of my life with you."

"Let's just take this one day at a time. No deals. No promises."

He meant to protest, but she kissed him again, pressing her body to his and distracting him with the savory texture of her tongue. His pulse quickened as he responded in kind, pulling her close and caressing her back. He slid his hands down and squeezed her firm bottom. She made a soft sound in her throat and moved against him, stirring him through his clothes.

After an endless time, he pulled away just far enough to gaze down at her. "Will you stay with me tonight? I want to fall asleep with you, then wake in the morning to make love to you again."

"Yes, I'll stay." She tugged on his shirt and he slipped it off with one smooth motion.

She ran her hands over his torso tracing the valleys where muscle met bone as he unbuttoned her blouse. He swept the shirt open, then cupped her breasts through her bra. Moaning softly, he buried his face in her cleavage as he kneaded her.

How he'd missed the feel of her.

"So beautiful," he whispered against her flesh.

His thumbs pushed aside the lacy cups and he nuzzled a path to first one nipple, then the next, feasting on her with the steady pull of his mouth. Liquid heat spread through her veins. She moaned as he suckled her, then drew back to blow on the hardened peak.

They helped each other out of the remainder of their clothes, tossing garments aside to stroke and fondle as they pleased. She found his male nipples and teased them, rolling them between her fingers until he could hardly bear the intense sensation. It was almost a relief when she pushed him to his back, then straddled him and kissed his eyes shut. He inhaled her scent as she moved over him placing kisses at his crown, forehead, then throat.

Nudging her legs apart with his knee, he slipped his hand along her thigh to the slick folds of her femininity. She nuzzled his throat as he traced her clit, strumming it to a straining point. Then he slid two fingers into her welcoming heat and stroked her until she raised her head and moaned.

She moved away from him, sliding down his body to kiss the center of his chest, her mouth warm and soft. She paused there long enough for him to trace his hands over her back, then she placed another lingering kiss on his belly before slipping her hand to his cock. When her fingers closed over him, he shut his eyes and let the sensations take him.

They both reached for the nightstand drawer at the same time, and he fumbled with the condom. She helped to ready him with frustrated groans, until she slid over him and he pressed up into her, her warmth and vibrancy gloving him, sending excited tendrils of heat flowing through him.

Time suspended as she rode him, and he let his gaze travel over her flushed face, the pink tips of her breasts and the joining of their bodies, her skin translucent as the tension coiled through his body, bringing him closer to climax.

Her mouth formed a silent cry as she shuddered and her orgasm claimed her. She fell across him, her hair fanning across his face and her breath whispering across his cheek as a rainbow of light burst all around him and he came deep inside her.

"I'VE MADE A DECISION." NIKKI tucked a loose strand of hair behind her ear and waited until Dylan glanced up from his task of massaging lotion into her arm.

They'd had a beautiful night of loving and a languorous morning of more loving, followed by a soak in the tub and now this liberal pampering of every inch of her body. Who was she to complain if he wanted to spoil her?

"This is serious," she said as her towel slipped and his gaze slid to the exposed curve of her breast. She adjusted the towel and cleared her throat. "Now pay attention."

"Nikki, love, you are my total focus today. Your wish is my command."

"Good. I'll need your cooperation for this."

"Just name it. I aim to please."

"Okay. I want you to release me from the contract on this house."

He stared at her in silence a moment, his forehead crinkling. "I don't understand."

"You can't sell this house, Dylan."

"But I have. To you."

"Then let's undo it. It isn't too late. We haven't closed yet. And I don't want to buy it anymore."

He straightened. "Why not? This is a great house. I mean, a *really* great house. You won't find any others like it anywhere."

"Exactly."

His frown deepened. "Nikki, I think I get what you're doing here, but it's okay. It's important to you to establish your own place, right?"

"Yes, but I can find another place. This is *your* place. You dreamed it. You designed it. You created it. As much as I want this absolutely incredible house, I could never want it the way you do. It's yours, Dylan. I couldn't stand to see you sell it, not when I know what it means to you. Especially now that you're studying to be an architect."

The blue of his eyes darkened. "I don't know what to say."

"Just say you'll release me. You promised to cooperate."

"If I agree—and I'm not saying yet that I am—what will you do? Where will you live?"

She shrugged. "I can always stay in my apartment with my sisters. Who knows, maybe I'll find another house by then."

"You'll never find another house like this."

"If you do say so yourself."

"I say so."

"But I'm sure I can find something I'll like almost as much. And I'll be able to live with myself, to boot— which I would *not* be able to do if I forced you to go through with this sale."

"Nikki—"

"I'm not going to change my mind and I can be very stubborn. You know, I think the seal on that fridge could be a deal breaker."

"Sweetheart—"

"And you know you'll need my help redoing the whole place now that you have most of it cleared out and ready to renovate."

"I like the basic structure. We're just talking new wallpaper and paint, maybe some new molding here or there."

"And you'll need new furniture. You cannot have Steven and Rebecca over for dinner and not have any dining room furniture."

"I still have the kitchen set."

"You need to fill that dining room. And the formal living room is empty, as well. And there are the bedrooms upstairs. You need to do something with the bathrooms. I'll get Erin's advice. We need to make a list. Do you have paper and pen?"

"I'll make the list, thank you. This is my place, and this time around *I* choose everything."

She smiled and threw her arms around him. "You agree then?"

"Only if you promise to help. This could take weeks, maybe even months. We'll have to work every night and weekends, too—"

"I work at the clinic Saturday mornings."

"Then you'll have to make it up to me by, say, sharing your luscious body with me at every opportunity."

"I think I can manage that."

"Good. You'll need to move your things back in. No sense in you having to run home all the time for clothes."

"Well, I might want to say hello to my sisters once in a while. There's a slight possibility they will miss me."

"Invite them over. I hate that I didn't get to meet your sisters that day we stopped by to pick up your things."

"Really? You wanted to meet them then?"

"Let's plan a big dinner party when we're done. We'll invite your entire family—anyone you think I should meet—and Steven and Becca, too. We'll concentrate on the dining room first."

She smiled at him, warmth expanding her chest. "*We* will?"

"You bet. This was your idea, so you're in this right along with me. This is definitely a 'we' project. Can you handle that?"

"Oh, yeah, I can handle it."

"I'll be right back." He kissed her soundly on the cheek, then moved to rummage in the nightstand.

Sitting back, she let his excitement infect her. They'd done it. They'd made it to the level of plural pronouns. For now, all was right in the world.

17

DYLAN STARED AT THE SWIPE of paint on the wall. "It's pink."

"It's sandalwood, and you liked it in the store."

"It wasn't pink in the store."

"It isn't pink, and this is a spare bedroom, so what does it matter? Are you planning on having pink-hating overnight guests anytime soon?"

"Sandalwood-hating, and no, I don't have any friends or family dying to visit, except Steven and Becca, who wouldn't need to spend the night. Did I really pick that color?"

"You did."

"What were you doing to distract me at the time?"

She wiggled her eyebrows. "I'll never tell."

He scooped one arm around her and pulled her to his side. "Maybe you could show me."

"After we finish painting."

"But we just started."

She brandished her roller at him. "Then you should get busy."

He let her go and dipped his own roller into the tray. "Slave driver."

"See, that spot is drying much darker." She cocked her head. "It's not so bad. Not so pink."

He grunted in reply and rolled a swatch of wall.

"If you hate it, then we'll redo it." She shrugged. "I should still be around for that."

"Oh, you'll be around, miss. I'm not letting you go anywhere. You didn't start me renovating my entire house just to bail on me."

She was quiet a moment as they rolled the walls, then she paused to dip her roller in the tray. "Dylan, you understand that I don't have any choice in how this plays out."

The serious tone of her voice had him turning to her, his stomach tightening. "What do you mean?"

"I mean us, this relationship. I don't have a say-so in when or how it ends."

"Of course you do. We both do. And as far as I'm concerned, we don't need to be having any conversations on ending things."

"But we do. Don't you see? It's part of this gift or curse or whatever you want to call it. I never had a choice before. They all ended and I had no control over it."

He stared at her a minute. It had never occurred to him to doubt her gift. He had felt her magic from the start. He'd known from the moment he laid eyes on her that she was somehow different. "Look, I refuse to believe that this thing is bigger than the both of us. If we decide to remain together, then we're together. End of story."

"But you won't want to stay, Dylan."

"That is bull. What would make me want to leave you?"

She gave a short, sad laugh. "You'll be healed and you'll want to go out and conquer the world…and I'll be left behind."

He dropped his roller, took hers from her and laid it in the tray, then took her in his arms. "Baby, I am not going anywhere. I want to be with you. Nothing's going to change that. And as far as this whole healing thing goes, I've never felt better. I think you've worked your charms on me, mission completed, and here I am. I haven't gone anywhere."

"You *are* very nearly healed. It's why I bring this up."

"Very nearly? I'm strong as an ox. I'm happy." He sobered and met her gaze. "I don't feel the darkness closing in on me the way it did before I met you."

"But a part of it is still there."

He frowned. "What do you mean?"

"I sense it. I feel it."

"You sense it?"

"I'm empathic. It's part of the gift."

"You can feel if someone needs healing?"

"Yes. With you I could feel this great sadness when we first met. You've worked through a vast amount of it, but it's like there's this shadow still." She placed her hand over his heart. "Here."

Was she right? "I'm sure everyone has a little something they're carrying around."

"I suppose."

"I think redoing this house has been a great testament to the progress I'm making in…letting go of my old life."

"It is. You've lightened with every little project we complete."

"So you think that we'll finish up this room and suddenly I won't want to be with you anymore?" His frustration flared into anger. "You think I'm only with you because of this healing you give me—that I'm using you in some way and when I'm through with you I'll want to discard you?"

Tears welled in her eyes and his gut twisted. "I'm sorry, baby, this is so frustrating. Here I'm thinking things are moving right along with us. I've gotten you to mostly move in with me. I think we're getting a good groove on, and you hit me with this things-could-suddenly-end and it's-out-of-our-control speech. It's a bit much to swallow."

"It's the way it's always been. You won't be able to help how you feel. You think you care about me now, but I'm telling you that will change."

"No…it won't. I don't know about this shadow, but I am a new man, thanks to you." He inhaled, then blew out the breath as he took her hands in his. "I care so much about you and it has been heaven having you here with me. What I really want is for you to make this your home, too. You don't need to go out house hunting, Nikki. This house needs you. I need you."

"I don't know what to say."

"Say yes."

"But I am here. I have clothes in the closet and my toothbrush by the sink. For all practical purposes, I am living here."

"It isn't enough. I want you to move all of your things in. I want you to be here long-term, not temporarily like you are now. I need more. I need to feel connected—a part of something. I want that something to be you."

"I can't make plans like that, Dylan. It isn't fair for you to ask me. You don't understand. We're on borrowed time here. I have never had a relationship last this long."

"I'm supposed to believe that? What kind of idiots were you dating?"

She lifted her chin. "No one else has ever wanted me past the healing."

"I am not like those other men. I want you. I am not suddenly going to stop wanting you. I'm sorry that you may have been hurt like that in the past, but it is unfair for you to punish me for something I didn't do."

"I'm not punishing you."

"Then make this your home, Nikki. Bring your sisters. There's plenty of room here, and I know how much they mean to you. I'm sure I'll love them. Hopefully they'll like me, too."

Tears swam in her eyes and he gritted his teeth to keep from roaring his frustration. "I can't. I'm sorry," she said. "I'm here for now and I will stay as long as you need me, as long as you want me. But we have to take this one day at a time."

"Well, I guess I'll take what I can get at this point." He turned from her and picked up his roller. Somehow, someway, he'd convince her to stay.

A SURPRISINGLY COOL BREEZE caught Nikki as she stepped into the courtyard. She smiled and inhaled the fresh scent of flowers. Dylan's voice drifted to her through the open door as he sang off-key to a song on the CD player.

Smiling, she left the door open so she could hear him and carried her shears and vase to the stand of wildflowers near the rock garden. Humming softly to the tune, she clipped an assortment of the golden, orange and red blooms, then arranged them in her vase one by one.

The doorbell rang, its musical gong echoing through the house. Dylan's singing stopped and the murmur of voices drifted through the open door. A familiar feminine laugh caught Nikki's attention and she rose in spite of herself to move closer to the sound.

"I was hoping I'd catch you alone." There was no mistaking Evelyn's voice. "I won't take much of your time. I see you're busy. The place is looking great. Very different."

"I'm finally making this house mine."

"Oh, so you'll be living here with Nikki?"

"She's backed out of the contract. The sale is off."

"So the two of you aren't planning anything long-term then?"

"Not that it's any of your business, but we're not planning anything." Aggravation rang clearly in his voice.

Nikki cringed. Was he angry because she refused to make any plans with him or because Evelyn had butted her nose into their business? Either way, Nikki still couldn't make him any promises.

"Dylan, I know you were upset with me for inviting her to the gala—"

"You were way out of line."

"I know, and I'm truly sorry. I'd like to make it up to you somehow."

"There's no need."

"I've come to make peace. Not just for myself but for your parents, too. They're really unhappy about this rift."

"Unhappy or pissed off?"

"Well, you know them. The two kind of go hand in hand."

"Did they send you?"

"No…not really, though they encouraged me to come. I have their full blessing."

She paused and Nikki chided herself for eavesdropping. Tess's bad habit had rubbed off on her. She reached for the handle to pull the door shut.

"The truth is that I've always been wild about you, Dylan."

Nikki's hand froze on the knob. She stood listening with her entire being. So Evelyn *did* want Dylan for herself.

"Evelyn—"

"Always, for as long as I remember. I broke things off with Nick. It wasn't fair to him. I went as far as I did with him because I'd hoped it would jolt you into realizing your true feelings. It upset you to see me with him. You can't deny it. I saw it in your eyes that night we stopped by and told you about our engagement."

Nikki held her breath. Dylan had been upset about Evelyn's engagement?

"I'm not going to deny that it bothered me, but—"

"I knew it."

"No, it isn't what you think."

"I could make you so happy, Dylan. I know you. I'm your kind of people. You can't deny who you are. You won't be able to keep yourself cut off from your friends and family for much longer. You need us and, frankly, we need you."

Nikki closed the door. Good God, Evelyn was right. Maybe Dylan didn't have the prize family, but he himself had admitted he needed to feel connected. He already had a family he was a part of. Would mending his relationship with his parents bring him the peace he needed?

And by his own admission, he'd been upset about Evelyn's engagement. Whether he felt ready to take her up on her offer didn't really matter. As long as Nikki was around, Dylan wouldn't be open to another relationship. Granted, he wasn't likely to end up with Evelyn, but surely there were other decent women in their crowd.

Nikki closed her eyes. Could she live with herself if

she didn't free him to make the choice for himself? Slowly she opened the door and peered in. Music still blasted from the CD player, but neither Dylan nor Evelyn seemed to be around. She stepped into the foyer and glanced out the window beside the door. Her heart skipped a beat. They stood beside Evelyn's car, locked in an embrace.

"Well, there you go. He's on his way to conquer the world." With a sick feeling in her stomach, she climbed the stairs.

WHERE HAD NIKKI GONE? SHE'D been missing since sometime that afternoon. Dylan paced through the rooms of his house, his frustration welling. It was getting late and she wasn't answering her cell phone.

He shook his head at his own impatience. And she thought he would come to not want her anymore. She'd been missing for a couple of hours and he was jumping out of his skin waiting for her return.

The house was nearly done. He'd have to talk her into helping him shop for furniture. Yes, he wanted to make this house a place that reflected his tastes, his personality, but he wanted her to be comfortable here, too. He'd meant what he'd said about her moving in.

The stairs creaked as he headed up to the second floor. They had finished most of the work on this level. His gaze fell across the master bedroom door and he paused, frowning.

They hadn't touched that room. How had he missed

it? Somehow he had blotted that room from his mind. He'd hardly set foot in it since the night of the accident. He moved toward it and turned the knob.

The quiet of the house pressed down around him as he pushed through the door. He flipped the nearby switch, and light from the bedside table cast a soft glow along the walls. Funny how it could all look so familiar yet strange at the same time.

He moved to the dresser and fingered the hairbrush Kathy had used every morning and every night for as long as he could remember. When he'd gathered items for the yard sale, it hadn't occurred to him to trespass in this room that had been a sanctuary to her. Had he thought of it, would he have been able to disturb her most personal possessions?

Dust coated the bristles. He rubbed his fingers together and tried to picture her perched on the side of the bed, running the brush through her hair. He'd loved to sit back and watch the way the golden strands caught the light.

Slowly the memory surfaced and he could see her clearly—clearer than he'd envisioned her in all the time since she'd been gone. His chest swelled with all the love and tenderness he'd ever felt for her. His love for her was there. It hadn't died with her. But peace flowed through him, too—a peace he couldn't have known without Nikki.

It no longer hurt to think about Kathy.

He placed the brush back on the dresser, then searched in the closet until he found an empty hatbox.

Kathy had been a collector of many things. He smiled at the box as he lifted the lid.

The time had come to gather the rest of her belongings. He would pack them up, then store them away for another day. He needed to make room for the trappings of his new life.

DYLAN'S HEART POUNDED AS he stared at his open closet an hour later. Where could Nikki be? He turned his back on the empty hangers and faced the room. How could she have left? She'd put as much into this house over the past weeks as he had. Not only had she labored beside him, she'd put a little of herself in each room. She had inspired the jungle motif that played in the leafy border of this bedroom, in the luscious trees of the entry and the pewter panther in his study. This was as much her home now as it was his.

And, damn it, he wanted her here to share it with him.

He grabbed the phone off the nightstand and punched in her number. After four rings, her cell phone switched into her voice mail.

"Nikki, where are you? I turn around and you disappear. I…need to talk to you. I figured out what the shadow was and it's gone. I can feel it's gone and I still want you. And, damn it, I need you."

He hung up, feeling unsettled. Unsettled. That was it. Nikki wanted to feel settled down and, for some incomprehensible reason, she didn't think she could do that here. So what would she do?

She'd go back to square one and restart her search for a house.

Now where had he put Ginger's number?

18

NIKKI WALKED THROUGH THE house, trailing after Ginger, going through the motions: smiling at the hopeful owner, nodding in agreement to the little tidbits of information Ginger supplied, looking in each nook and cranny as though she were really interested. Why had she come? Her heart just wasn't in it.

She'd come to embrace the world. She'd been the one to leave this time, so why did her heart feel as though she'd torn it out herself and stomped on it?

Dylan didn't need her anymore. He had Evelyn now. He had the chance to reconcile with his family—find the connection and sense of belonging he'd been missing. She'd done the right thing to leave. It would be nice to get back to her apartment and see how Tess and Erin were faring.

Maybe she'd pay Maggie a visit at Sophie's. What was that mother of hers up to? Surely she had some new masterpiece to share. She missed her, actually missed her. Warmth filled Nikki's chest as she stood facing a walk-in closet filled with a stranger's belongings.

She loved Maggie. She loved her mother. With that

acknowledgment came the acceptance of her gift. In one peaceful moment Nikki found acceptance for it all—for the mother who had dragged them from home to home, lover to lover, and for the gift of healing she'd passed on to her daughters.

"So this is how to let go," she murmured.

Maggie was dating a new man but, by her own admission, was taking things slower this time—*savoring* it was how she'd put it. That had sparked an entire conversation on savoring men. Even Sophie had joined in.

Longing swelled in Nikki's heart. Oh, what a savory man Dylan was.

"So what do you think?" Ginger peered at her.

"Oh." Nikki glanced around the spacious bedroom. "It's nice."

"*Nice* is for aunts and birthday presents you wished you hadn't gotten."

"I'm sorry, Ginger. I was hoping we'd find something that would knock me off my feet, but I guess I'm just not in the mood to do this today."

"Wouldn't have anything to do with one hot ex-attorney we both know?"

Nikki stared at her a moment, not sure how to respond. "I have never been so turned around and clueless in my life."

"Love will do that to you."

Love? Nikki blinked. Of course, love—she did love Dylan, probably had for a long time. "Yes, I suppose it will. Can I ask you something?"

"Fire away. I've been married five times and loved deeply every time. I'm an expert."

"Is there any price too high to pay for that kind of love—you know, the kind that lifts you up, turns you around, then drops you like a roller coaster until you're all confused and can't imagine life without that person?"

"That's too easy. No, there is no price too high for that kind of love."

Ginger's cell phone rang from inside her purse. She excused herself to answer it, but her eyes widened and she motioned to Nikki. "Actually she's right here. Do you want me to put her on? Oh…okay, I'll see what I can do."

She rattled off an address that sounded vaguely familiar, then hung up and turned to Nikki, a smile lighting up her face. "That was him."

"Who?"

"Dylan. How many hot ex-attorneys do you know?"

"What did he want?"

"Well, *you* evidently."

"Why didn't he ask to talk to me?"

"I guess whatever he has to say, he wants to say in person. He's on his way."

"ARE YOU SURE YOU DON'T WANT me to stick around?" Ginger's gaze had that same hopeful appeal it had held earlier.

"I'm not so sure *I* want to stick around."

"Don't be silly. Of course you do. You have to at least

hear the man out." She raised her eyes to the sky. "To be young and in love again."

"You know, love knows no boundaries, Ginger. My mother falls in love at least once every few months. There's always hope."

"Hope won't even get me a cup of coffee." She straightened at the sound of squealing tires.

Dylan's car rounded the corner, then came to a screeching halt in front of them. Nikki turned to Ginger. "Thanks so much. I'm sorry about that first deal falling through, but I'll call you when I'm ready to start looking again."

Ginger nodded as Dylan stepped out of the car. "Hello, handsome." She winked at him as he moved beside Nikki.

"Ginger." He nodded to her.

A bird cawed overhead. Ginger stood smiling at them. The breeze teased around them. After a moment, she straightened. "Okay, then, guess I'll be going and leave you two youngsters alone…by yourselves…to discuss whatever it is that you might want to discuss. Although maybe you want to find a private spot to have this discussion instead of by the side of the street, where anyone passing by might be privy to your conversation…about whatever is so important that you had to come flying over here like a bat out of hell."

Nikki gave her a wide-eyed look. "Thank you, Ginger. You have a nice evening."

"Right. I'll just go ahead and leave now." With that

she waved her final goodbye, headed across the street to her car with a backward glance or two. Her engine fired and a moment later she was gone.

A lawn mower started somewhere in the distance and the scent of barbecue drifted on the breeze. Dylan toed a stone into the gutter. "You left me."

"Yes, I did."

His gaze pinned her. "Why?"

Why had she left? Her reasoning seemed jumbled and nonsensical standing here beside him, his virile presence overwhelming her senses, confusing the issues.

"Well?"

"You don't need me anymore, Dylan."

"The hell I don't."

"What about Evelyn?"

"What *about* Evelyn?"

She shrugged. "She may not have always had the best intentions, but no one is all bad. I'm sure there's something good in her. She's your people. She's in love with you. I heard you talking. I saw you embracing."

"First of all, that was her talking, not me. If you'd listened to the whole conversation, you'd know that hug was me telling her goodbye and wishing her well. I forgive her for anything she may have done and I wish her well. Mainly I wish her out of my life."

"Are you sure?"

"Maybe I tried to be her people—my parents' people—for a while, but I was really never one of them. Thank God they sent me away, so they could be less of an influence on me while I was growing up." He gripped her arms and turned her toward him. "She's not my people and she doesn't love me. She loves the idea of me—the image I put out there all those years in my pathetic attempt to gain acceptance."

"But you want to feel connected. They're your family. How can you just turn your back on them? Maybe I encouraged it after that party, when they were so cold and bitter, but I was wrong. Family is family."

"I'm just taking a break from them. Let them miss me and appreciate me while I'm not around. I want to start a family of my own, have a couple of rug rats. Not because my mother will drop down on her knees and beg to be a part of her grandchildren's lives, but because I really want to have children of my own…with the woman I love."

He embraced her and pressed his forehead to hers. "With you."

"Dylan—"

He drew back far enough to make eye contact. "Wait. I'm not finished. I know this may be a lot to spring on you at once, but I'm feeling pretty good right now and it's all thanks to you. The shadow's gone.

"See?" His hand pressed the center of his chest. "I figured it out. There was this door I'd shut and forgotten about—both figuratively and literally. I never said goodbye to her. I just closed the door and I never really dealt with it."

She smoothed her hand over his. It was true. The darkness had left him. "So it *was* Kathy."

"I had to let her go. I didn't even realize I was holding on so tight. But I did it, Nikki. I opened that door and I looked through her things. I packed them up…and I said goodbye."

"That's good. I'm happy for you."

"So." He cocked his head.

"So."

"It's really hot out here."

"Miami in July."

"Will you marry me, Nikki? Have a family with me?"

Her heart swelled. "It *is* a lot to spring on me, especially when I couldn't commit to living with you."

"Okay, we can start there. Baby steps, if that's what you need. As long as you're with me, I can be a patient man. Just promise me you'll consider it."

"Ultimately nothing's changed."

"Sure it has. I'm healed and I still want you, like I said I would."

"I don't understand. I don't know what this means." She shook her head. "You're supposed to be off conquering the world."

"But I do want to conquer the world. I just want you by my side while I do it." He straightened. "So what does this mean in terms of your gift?"

"I'm not sure, but if I stay with you, it could mean that I lose my gift."

His expression fell and sadness again swirled around him, though it was a sadness of a different sort. "I hadn't thought of that and I won't ask it of you."

Could she give up the gift? It had been more of a curse than a blessing, except when it came to Dylan. If she couldn't be with Dylan, would she want to share her gift with another man? The answer came to her with a certainty she couldn't deny.

"You don't have to ask me to give it up," she said. "I do it freely."

"Nikki, are you sure?"

She gazed into his eyes and his love radiated out to her, enveloped her. How could she ever have doubted it? "Yes, I'm sure. I love you, Dylan."

He pulled her to him and his mouth closed over hers, his tongue stealing in to dance with hers, stroking, teasing, evoking that heat. After an endless time, she pulled back and fanned herself. "Oh my, it *is* awfully warm out here."

He grinned. "Miami in July. I know a place that stays pretty well refrigerated. Want to go?"

"How *do* you afford the electric bill?"

"Well, I'm now a starving wannabe architect. I may have to take up a collection."

"Are you really starving?" She eyed him with skepticism. "You look hearty and hale to me."

"Okay, so maybe I'm not starving, except perhaps for you."

"Well, then, let's go enjoy the feast of a lifetime."

"It *is* cold in here." Nikki shivered as Dylan pressed her to the wall and nibbled a path along her neck.

They had barely made it through the door, but at least they were home. He murmured her name as he slipped her top over her head. His breath fanned across her chest and he unfastened her bra with the flick of his fingers.

"Oh…that's nice." She rolled her head back as he suckled her with abandon, teasing one nipple into a hard peak with the steady stroke of his tongue while his fingers played havoc over the other.

"Look at you." He leaned back to gaze at his handiwork.

Warmth filled her at the sight of the beaded tips, wet with his loving. Then she shivered again as a cool blast of air hit her. "Okay, if I'm going shirtless, then so are you."

He let her yank off his shirt, then it was no holds barred as they stripped each other, clothes flying and temperatures rising. As he knelt to help her step from her panties, his breath brushed her triangle of hair. She shivered.

With a soft moan he nuzzled her there, parting her thighs and bracing her leg over his shoulder. His mouth took her with a hunger that left her weak, breathless. He laved every inch of her, taking his time to trace each fold, to circle her clit with the pointed tip of his tongue.

Her blood warmed and liquid pooled from her. He drank from her desire, telling her with the stroke of his tongue, the touch of his hands, that he indeed wanted her.

She closed her eyes and basked in his giving. The heat and tension built inside her until she moaned and moved against him, straining for release.

He granted it to her in a moment of blinding ecstasy as she came against his mouth, her hands buried in his hair. Still he knelt before her, his lips on her, calming her, caressing her most private center with gentle kisses.

At long last he rose and took her hand. On unsteady legs she followed him, not to the bedroom they had shared but upstairs to the room at the end of the hall. She stopped as they neared the open door.

"Dylan, are you sure?"

He cupped her face and his love flowed over her. "I promise, there are no ghosts."

She nodded and he led her inside. Light spilled across the walls from a large bay window. She glanced around, amazed at how much he had transformed the space in the short expanse of the afternoon. Not a trace of Kathy remained.

The furniture had been removed and a large futon occupied the spot that had housed the bed. Dylan led her to the soft cushions and she lay down with him. All thoughts of the room and its former occupant fled as he touched her, kissed her, stroked her to the brink of climax again.

At some point he readied himself and slipped into her when she thought she'd die of need. He filled her, stretched her and touched her in all the right places, in all the right ways. He moved in and out of her with long, smooth motions. She braced her feet against the futon and met him thrust for thrust, and when his hand fisted in her hair and his body tensed in orgasm, she came along with him, carried away in a rainbow of light and sensation.

When his breathing calmed and he'd eased his weight off her, he traced the line of her cheek. "So do I take this as a yes?"

She glanced at him in question and he grinned. "Are we taking baby steps? Are you ready to move in on a trial basis?"

"Oh, actually the answer to that would be no."

"No?"

"No. If we're going to have any rug rats, we should definitely commit for the long haul."

A smile burst across his face. "Are you saying yes, you'll marry me?"

"And have your children. Granted, I think *that* we should do in steps. Have one and see how it goes before we commit to another."

"Oh, you'll want at least two."

"Maybe."

"So maybe we should go ahead and give it a try."

"Give what a try?"

"Getting pregnant."

She rubbed his nose with hers, then leaned back to see him better. "Let's wait a while for that. I want you to myself for now, and with my luck, you'll be some one-shot wonder."

A slow smile broke across his face. "Well, I don't see anything wrong with that."

"No." She smiled back at him. "Maybe being a one-shot wonder isn't a bad thing at all."

* * * * *

Watch for Tess McClellan's story
SO MANY MEN...
the second story in Dorie Graham's
SEXUAL HEALING
miniseries! On sale September 2005
from Harlequin Blaze.

HARLEQUIN® *Blaze*™

Where were you when the lights went out?

Shane Walker was seducing his best friend in:

#194 NIGHT MOVES

by **Julie Kenner** July 2005

Adam and Mallory were rekindling
the flames of first love in:

#200 WHY NOT TONIGHT?

by **Jacquie D'Alessandro** August 2005

Simon Thackery was professing his love...
to his best friend's fiancée in:

#206 DARING IN THE DARK

by **Jennifer LaBrecque** September 2005

**24 Hours:
BLACKOUT**

If you enjoyed what you just read,
then we've got an offer you can't resist!

Take 2 bestselling
love stories FREE!
Plus get a FREE surprise gift!

Clip this page and mail it to Harlequin Reader Service®

IN U.S.A.
3010 Walden Ave.
P.O. Box 1867
Buffalo, N.Y. 14240-1867

IN CANADA
P.O. Box 609
Fort Erie, Ontario
L2A 5X3

YES! Please send me 2 free Harlequin® Blaze™ novels and my free surprise gift. After receiving them, if I don't wish to receive anymore, I can return the shipping statement marked cancel. If I don't cancel, I will receive 6 brand-new novels each month, before they're available in stores! In the U.S.A., bill me at the bargain price of $3.99 plus 25¢ shipping and handling per book and applicable sales tax, if any*. In Canada, bill me at the bargain price of $4.47 plus 25¢ shipping and handling per book and applicable taxes**. That's the complete price and a savings of at least 10% off the cover prices—what a great deal! I understand that accepting the 2 free books and gift places me under no obligation ever to buy any books. I can always return a shipment and cancel at any time. Even if I never buy another book from Harlequin, the 2 free books and gift are mine to keep forever.

151 HDN D7ZZ
351 HDN D72D

Name	(PLEASE PRINT)	
Address	Apt.#	
City	State/Prov.	Zip/Postal Code

Not valid to current Harlequin® Blaze™ subscribers.

Want to try two free books from another series?
Call 1-800-873-8635 or visit www.morefreebooks.com.

* Terms and prices subject to change without notice. Sales tax applicable in N.Y.
** Canadian residents will be charged applicable provincial taxes and GST.
 All orders subject to approval. Offer limited to one per household.
 ® and ™ are registered trademarks owned and used by the trademark owner and/or its licensee.

BLZ05   ©2005 Harlequin Enterprises Limited.

brings you an unforgettable
new miniseries from author

Linda Conrad

The Gypsy Inheritance

A secret legacy unleashes passion...and promises.

Scandal and seduction go hand in hand as three
powerful men receive unexpected gifts....

SEDUCTION
BY THE BOOK

August 2005
Silhouette Desire #1673

REFLECTED PLEASURES

September 2005
Silhouette Desire #1679

A SCANDALOUS
MELODY

October 2005
Silhouette Desire #1684

Available at your favorite retail outlet.

HARLEQUIN®
Blaze™

COMING NEXT MONTH

#201 UNZIPPED? Karen Kendall
The Man-Handlers, Bk. 2

What happens when a beautiful image consultant meets a stereotypical computer guy? Explosive sex, of course. Shannon Shane is stunned how quickly she falls for her client, Hal Underwood. As the hottie inside emerges, she just can't keep her hands to herself.

#202 SO MANY MEN... Dorie Graham
Sexual Healing, Bk. 2

Sex with Tess McClellan is the best experience Mason Davies has had. Apparently all of her old lovers think so, too, because they're everywhere. Mason would leave, except that he's addicted. He'll just have to convince her she'll always be satisfied with him!

#203 SEX & SENSIBILITY Shannon Hollis

After sensitive Tessa Nichols has a vision of a missing girl, she and former cop Griffin Knox—who falsely arrested her two years ago—work to find her. Ultimately, Tessa has to share with him every spicy, red-hot vision she has, and soon separating fantasy from reality beomes a job perk neither of them anticipated....

#204 HER BODY OF WORK Marie Donovan

Undercover DEA agent Marco Flores was used to expecting the unexpected. But he never dreamed he'd end up on the run—and posing as a model. A nude model! He'd taken the job to protect his brother, but he soon discovered there were undeniable perks. Like having his sculptress, sexy Rey Martinson, wind up as uncovered as he was...

#205 SIMPLY SEX Dawn Atkins

Who knew that guys using matchmakers were so hot? Kylie Falls didn't until she met Cole Sullivan. Too bad she's only his stand-in date. But the sparks between them beg to be explored in a sizzling, delicious fling. And they both know this is temporary...right?

#206 DARING IN THE DARK Jennifer LaBrecque
24 Hours: Blackout, Bk. 3

Simon Thackeray almost has it all—good looks, a good job and good friends. The only thing he's missing is the one woman he wants more than his next breath—the woman who, unfortunately, is engaged to his best friend. It looks hopeless—until a secret confession and a twenty-four-hour blackout give him the chance to prove he's the better man....

www.eHarlequin.com

HBCNM0805